Joseph Addison

Essays and Tales

Joseph Addison

Essays and Tales

ISBN/EAN: 9783337120849

Printed in Europe, USA, Canada, Australia, Japan

Cover: Foto ©Andreas Hilbeck / pixelio.de

More available books at **www.hansebooks.com**

CASSELL'S NATIONAL LIBRARY.

ESSAYS AND TALES.

BY

JOSEPH ADDISON.

CASSELL & COMPANY, Limited:

LONDON, PARIS, NEW YORK & MELBOURNE.

1888.

INTRODUCTION.

THE sixty-fourth volume of this Library contains those papers from the *Tatler* which were especially associated with the imagined character of ISAAC BICKERSTAFF, who was the central figure in that series; and in the twenty-ninth volume there is a similar collection of papers relating to the Spectator Club and SIR ROGER DE COVERLEY, who was the central figure in Steele and Addison's *Spectator.* Those volumes contained, no doubt, some of the best Essays of Addison and Steele. But in the *Tatler* and *Spectator* are full armouries of the wit and wisdom of these two writers, who summoned into life the army of the Essayists, and led it on to kindly war against the forces of Ill-temper and Ignorance. Envy, Hatred, Malice, and all their first cousins of the family of Uncharitableness, are captains under those two commanders-in-chief, and we can little afford to dismiss from the field two of the stoutest combatants against them. In this volume it is only Addison who speaks; and in another volume, presently to follow, there will be the voice of Steele.

The two friends differed in temperament and in many of the outward signs of character; but these two little books will very distinctly show how wholly they agreed as to essentials. For Addison, Literature had a charm of its own; he delighted in distinguishing the finer graces of good style, and he drew from the truths of life the principles of taste in writing. For Steele, Literature was the life itself; he loved a true book for the soul he found in it. So he agreed with Addison in judgment. But the six papers on " Wit," the two papers on "Chevy Chase," contained in this volume; the eleven papers on " Imagination," and the papers on " Paradise Lost," which may be given in some future volume; were in a form of study for which Addison was far more apt than Steele. Thus as fellow-workers they gave a breadth to the character of *Tatler* and *Spectator* that could have been produced by neither of them, singly.

The reader of this volume will never suppose that the artist's pleasure in good art and in analysis of its constituents removes him from direct enjoyment of the life about him; that he misses a real contact with all the world gives that is worth his touch. Good art is but nature, studied with love trained to the most delicate perception; and the good criticism in which the spirit of an artist speaks is, like Addison's, calm, simple, and benign. Pope yearned to attack John Dennis, a rough critic of the day, who had attacked his " Essay on Criticism." Addison had discouraged a very small assault of words. When Dennis attacked Addison's " Cato," Pope thought himself free to strike ; but Addison took occasion to express. through Steele, a serious regret that he had done so. True criticism may be affected. as Addison's was. by some bias in the canons of taste prevalent in the writer's time, but, as Addison's did in the Chevy-Chase papers, it will dissent from prevalent misapplications of them, and it can never associate perception of the purest truth and beauty with petty arrogance, nor will it so speak as to give pain. When Wordsworth was remembering with love his mother's guidance of his childhood, and wished to suggest that there were mothers less wise in their ways, he was checked, he said, by the unwillingness to join thought of her "with any thought that looks at others' blame." So Addison felt towards his mother Nature, in literature and in life. He attacked nobody. With a light, kindly humour, that was never personal and never could give pain, he sought to soften the harsh lines of life, abate its follies, and inspire the temper that alone can overcome its wrongs.

Politics, in which few then knew how to think calmly and recognise the worth of various opinion, Steele and Addison excluded from the pages of the *Spectator*. But the first paper in this volume is upon "Public Credit," and it did touch on the position of the country at a time when the shock of change caused by the Revolution of 1688-89, and also the strain of foreign war, were being severely felt.

H. M.

CONTENTS.

ESSAYS AND TALES.

PUBLIC CREDIT.

*— Quoi quisque ferè studio devinctus adhærct
Aut quibus in rebus multùm sumus antè morati
Atque in quô ratione fuit contenta magis mens,
In somnis eadem plerumque videmur obire.*
LUCR., iv. 959.

—What studies please, what most delight,
And fill men's thoughts, they dream 'them o'er at night.
CREECH.

IN one of my rambles, or rather speculations, I looked into the great hall where the bank is kept, and was not a little pleased to see the directors, secretaries, and clerks, with all the other members of that wealthy corporation, ranged in their several stations, according to the parts they act in that just and regular economy. This revived in my memory the many discourses which I had both read and heard concerning the decay of public credit, with the methods of restoring it; and which, in my opinion, have always been defective, because they have always been made with an eye to separate interests and party principles.

The thoughts of the day gave my mind employment

for the whole night; so that I fell insensibly into a
kind of methodical dream, which disposed all my
contemplations into a vision, or allegory, or what else
the reader shall please to call it.

Methoughts I returned to the great hall, where I
had been the morning before; but to my surprise, instead of the company that I left there, I saw, towards
the upper end of the hall, a beautiful virgin, seated on
a throne of gold. Her name, as they told me, was
Public Credit. The walls, instead of being adorned
with pictures and maps, were hung with many Acts of
Parliament written in golden letters. At the upper
end of the hall was the Magna Charta, with the Act of
Uniformity on the right hand, and the Act of Toleration
on the left. At the lower end of the hall was the Act
of Settlement, which was placed full in the eye of the
virgin that sat upon the throne. Both the sides of
the hall were covered with such Acts of Parliament as
had been made for the establishment of public funds.
The lady seemed to set an unspeakable value upon
these several pieces of furniture, insomuch that she
often refreshed her eye with them, and often smiled
with a secret pleasure as she looked upon them; but,
at the same time, showed a very particular uneasiness
if she saw anything approaching that might hurt them.
She appeared, indeed, infinitely timorous in all her
behaviour: and whether it was from the delicacy of
her constitution, or that she was troubled with vapours,

as I was afterwards told by one who I found was none
of her well-wishers, she changed colour and startled
at everything she heard. She was likewise, as I afterwards found, a greater valetudinarian than any I had
ever met with, even in her own sex, and subject to
such momentary consumptions, that in the twinkling
of an eye, she would fall away from the most florid
complexion and the most healthful state of body, and
wither into a skeleton. Her recoveries were often as
sudden as her decays, insomuch that she would revive
in a moment out of a wasting distemper, into a habit
of the highest health and vigour.

I had very soon an opportunity of observing these
quick turns and changes in her constitution. There
sat at her feet a couple of secretaries, who received
every hour letters from all parts of the world, which
the one or the other of them was perpetually reading
to her, and according to the news she heard, to which
she was exceedingly attentive, she changed colour, and
discovered many symptoms of health or sickness.

Behind the throne was a prodigious heap of bags of
money, which were piled upon one another so high that
they touched the ceiling. The floor on her right hand
and on her left was covered with vast sums of gold
that rose up in pyramids on either side of her. But
this I did not so much wonder at, when I heard, upon
inquiry, that she had the same virtue in her touch,
which the poets tell us a Lydian king was formerly

possessed of; and that she could convert whatever she pleased into that precious metal.

After a little dizziness, and confused hurry of thought, which a man often meets with in a dream, methoughts the hall was alarmed, the doors flew open, and there entered half a dozen of the most hideous phantoms that I had ever seen, even in a dream, before that time. They came in two by two, though matched in the most dissociable manner, and mingled together in a kind of dance. It would be tedious to describe their habits and persons; for which reason I shall only inform my reader, that the first couple were Tyranny and Anarchy; the second were Bigotry and Atheism; the third, the Genius of a commonwealth and a young man of about twenty-two years of age, whose name I could not learn. He had a sword in his right hand, which in the dance he often brandished at the Act of Settlement; and a citizen, who stood by me, whispered in my ear, that he saw a spunge in his left hand. The dance of so many jarring natures put me in mind of the sun, moon, and earth, in the *Rehearsal,* that danced together for no other end but to eclipse one another.

The reader will easily suppose, by what has been before said, that the lady on the throne would have been almost frighted to distraction, had she seen but any one of the spectres: what then must have been her condition when she saw them all in a body? She fainted, and died away at the sight.

Et neque jam color est misto candore rubori ;
Nec vigor, et vires, et quæ modò visa placebant ;
Nec corpus remanet—.

OVID, *Met.* iii. 491.

—Her spirits faint,
Her blooming cheeks assume a pallid teint,
And scarce her form remains.

There was as great a change in the hill of money-bags and the heaps of money, the former shrinking and falling into so many empty bags, that I now found not above a tenth part of them had been filled with money.

The rest, that took up the same space and made the same figure as the bags that were really filled with money, had been blown up with air, and called into my memory the bags full of wind, which Homer tells us his hero received as a present from Æolus. The great heaps of gold on either side the throne now appeared to be only heaps of paper, or little piles of notched sticks, bound up together in bundles, like Bath faggots.

Whilst I was lamenting this sudden desolation that had been made before me, the whole scene vanished. In the room of the frightful spectres, there now entered a second dance of apparitions, very agreeably matched together, and made up of very amiable phantoms: the first pair was Liberty with Monarchy at her right hand; the second was Moderation leading in Religion; and the third, a person whom I had

never seen, with the Genius of Great Britain. At the
first entrance, the lady revived; the bags swelled to
their former bulk; the piles of faggots and heaps of
paper changed into pyramids of guineas: and, for my
own part, I was so transported with joy that I awaked,
though I must confess I would fain have fallen asleep
again to have closed my vision, if I could have done it.

HOUSEHOLD SUPERSTITIONS.

Somnia, terrores magicos, miracula, sagas,
Nocturnos lemures, portentaque Thessala rides?
HOR., *Ep.* ii. 2, 208.

Visions and magic spells, can you despise,
And laugh at witches, ghosts, and prodigies?

GOING yesterday to dine with an old acquaintance,
I had the misfortune to find his whole family very
much dejected. Upon asking him the occasion of it,
he told me that his wife had dreamt a very strange
dream the night before, which they were afraid por-
tended some misfortune to themselves or to their
children. At her coming into the room, I observed a
settled melancholy in her countenance, which I should
have been troubled for, had I not heard from whence
it proceeded. We were no sooner sat down, but, after
having looked upon me a little while, "My dear,"

says she, turning to her husband, "you may now see
the stranger that was in the candle last night." Soon
after this, as they began to talk of family affairs, a
little boy at the lower end of the table told her that he
was to go into join-hand on Thursday. "Thursday!"
says she. "No, child ; if it please God, you shall not
begin upon Childermas-day; tell your writing-master
that Friday will be soon enough." I was reflecting
with myself on the oddness of her fancy, and wonder-
ing that anybody would establish it as a rule, to lose a
day in every week. In the midst of these my musings,
she desired me to reach her a little salt upon the point
of my knife, which I did in such a trepidation and
hurry of obedience that I let it drop by the way ; at
which she immediately startled, and said it fell towards
her. Upon this I looked very blank ; and observing
the concern of the whole table, began to consider
myself, with some confusion, as a person that had
brought a disaster upon the family. The lady, however, recovering herself after a little space, said to her
husband with a sigh, " My dear, misfortunes never
come single." My friend, I found, acted but an under
part at his table ; and, being a man of more good-nature
than understanding, thinks himself obliged to fall in
with all the passions and humours of his yoke-fellow.
"Do not you remember, child," says she, "that the
pigeon-house fell the very afternoon that our careless
wench spilt the salt upon the table?"—"Yes," says

he, "my dear; and the next post brought us an account of the battle of Almanza." The reader may guess at the figure I made, after having done all this mischief. I despatched my dinner as soon as I could, with my usual taciturnity; when, to my utter confusion, the lady seeing me quitting my knife and fork, and laying them across one another upon my plate, desired me that I would humour her so far as to take them out of that figure and place them side by side. What the absurdity was which I had committed I did not know, but I suppose there was some traditionary superstition in it; and therefore, in obedience to the lady of the house, I disposed of my knife and fork in two parallel lines, which is the figure I shall always lay them in for the future, though I do not know any reason for it.

It is not difficult for a man to see that a person has conceived an aversion to him. For my own part, I quickly found, by the lady's looks, that she regarded me as a very odd kind of fellow, with an unfortunate aspect: for which reason I took my leave immediately after dinner, and withdrew to my own lodgings. Upon my return home, I fell into a profound contemplation on the evils that attend these superstitious follies of mankind; how they subject us to imaginary afflictions, and additional sorrows, that do not properly come within our lot. As if the natural calamities of life were not sufficient for it, we turn the most indifferent circumstances into misfortunes, and suffer as much from trifling accidents as from real evils. I have known the shooting of a star spoil a night's rest; and have seen a man in love grow pale, and lose his appetite, upon the plucking of a merry-thought. A screech-owl at midnight has alarmed a family more than a band of robbers; nay, the voice of a cricket hath struck more terror than the roaring of a lion. There is nothing so inconsiderable which may not appear dreadful to an imagination that is filled with omens and prognostics: a rusty nail or a crooked pin shoot up into prodigies.

I remember I was once in a mixed assembly that was full of noise and mirth, when on a sudden an old woman unluckily observed there were thirteen of us in company. This remark struck a panic terror into several who were present, insomuch that one or two of the ladies were going to leave the room; but a friend of mine taking notice that one of our female companions was big with child, affirmed there were fourteen in the room, and that, instead of portending one of the company should die, it plainly foretold one of them should be born. Had not my friend found this expedient to break the omen, I question not but half the women in the company would have fallen sick that very night.

An old maid that is troubled with the vapours produces infinite disturbances of this kind among her friends and neighbours. I know a maiden aunt of a great family, who is one of these antiquated Sibyls, that forebodes and prophesies from one end of the year to the other. She is always seeing apparitions and hearing death-watches; and was the other day almost frighted out of her wits by the great house-dog that howled in the stable, at a time when she lay ill of the toothache. Such an extravagant cast of mind engages multitudes of people not only in impertinent terrors, but in supernumerary duties of life, and arises from that fear and ignorance which are natural to the soul of man. The horror with which we entertain the thoughts of death, or indeed of any future evil, and the uncertainty of its approach, fill a melancholy mind with innumerable apprehensions and suspicious, and consequently dispose it to the observation of such groundless prodigies and predictions. For as it is the chief concern of wise men to retrench the evils of life by the reasonings of philosophy, it is the employment of fools to multiply them by the sentiments of superstition.

For my own part, I should be very much troubled were I endowed with this divining quality, though it should inform me truly of everything that can befall me. I would not anticipate the relish of any happiness, nor feel the weight of any misery, before it actually arrives.

I know but one way of fortifying my soul against

these gloomy presages and terrors of mind; and that is, by securing to myself the friendship and protection of that Being who disposes of events and governs futurity. He sees, at one view, the whole thread of my existence, not only that part of it which I have already passed through, but that which runs forward into all the depths of eternity. When I lay me down to sleep, I recommend myself to His care; when I awake, I give myself up to His direction. Amidst all the evils that threaten me, I will look up to Him for help, and question not but He will either avert them, or turn them to my advantage. Though I know neither the time nor the manner of the death I am to die, I am not at all solicitous about it; because I am sure that He knows them both, and that He will not fail to comfort and support me under them.

OPERA LIONS.

Dic mihi, si fias tu leo, qualis eris!

MART., xii. 93.

Were you a lion, how would you behave?

THERE is nothing that of late years has afforded matter of greater amusement to the town than Signior Nicolini's combat with a lion in the Haymarket, which has been very often exhibited to the general satisfaction of most of the nobility and gentry in the kingdom of Great Britain. Upon the first rumour of this intended combat, it was confidently affirmed, and is still believed, by many in both galleries, that there would be a tame lion sent from the tower every opera night in order to be killed by Hydaspes. This report, though altogether groundless, so universally prevailed in the upper regions of the playhouse, that some of the most refined politicians in those parts of the audience gave it out in whisper that the lion was a cousin-german of the tiger who made his appearance in King William's days, and that the stage would be supplied with lions at the public expense during the whole session. Many likewise were the conjectures of the treatment which this lion was to meet with from the hands of Signior Nicolini: some supposed that he was to subdue him in recitativo, as Orpheus used to serve the wild beasts in his time, and afterwards to knock him on the head; some fancied that the lion would not pretend to lay his paws upon the hero, by reason of the received opinion that a lion will not hurt a virgin: several who pretended to have seen the opera in Italy, had informed their friends that the lion was to act a part in High Dutch, and roar twice or thrice to a thorough bass before he fell at the feet of Hydaspes. To clear up a matter that was so variously reported, I have made it my business to examine whether this pretended lion is really the savage he appears to be, or only a counterfeit.

But before I communicate my discoveries, I must
acquaint the reader that upon my walking behind the
scenes last winter, as I was thinking on something
else, I accidentally jostled against a monstrous animal
that extremely startled me, and, upon my nearer survey
of it, appeared to be a lion rampant. The lion, seeing
me very much surprised, told me, in a gentle voice, that
I might come by him if I pleased; "for," says he, " I
do not intend to hurt anybody." I thanked him very
kindly and passed by him, and in a little time after
saw him leap upon the stage and act his part with very
great applause. It has been observed by several that
the lion has changed his manner of acting twice or
thrice since his first appearance, which will not
seem strange when I acquaint my reader that the lion
has been changed upon the audience three several times.
The first lion was a candle-snuffer, who, being a fellow
of a testy, choleric temper, overdid his part, and would
not suffer himself to be killed so easily as he ought to
have done : besides, it was observed of him, that he
grew more surly every time he came out of the lion,
and having dropped some words in ordinary conversation, as if he had not fought his best, and that he
suffered himself to be thrown upon his back in the
scuffle, and that he would wrestle with Mr. Nicolini for
what he pleased, out of his lion's skin, it was thought
proper to discard him : and it is verily believed to this
day, that, had he been brought upon the stage another

time, he would certainly have done mischief. Besides, it was objected against the first lion, that he reared himself so high upon his hinder paws, and walked in so erect a posture, that he looked more like an old man than a lion.

The second lion was a tailor by trade, who belonged to the playhouse, and had the character of a mild and peaceable man in his profession. If the former was too furious, this was too sheepish for his part; inasmuch that, after a short modest walk upon the stage, he would fall at the first touch of Hydaspes, without grappling with him, and giving him an opportunity of showing his variety of Italian trips. It is said, indeed, that he once gave him a rip in his flesh-colour doublet: but this was only to make work for himself in his private character of a tailor. I must not omit that it was this second lion who treated me with so much humanity behind the scenes.

The acting lion at present is, as I am informed, a country gentleman, who does it for his diversion, but desires his name may be concealed. He says very handsomely, in his own excuse, that he does not act for gain; that he indulges an innocent pleasure in it, and that it is better to pass away an evening in this manner than in gaming and drinking: but at the same time says, with a very agreeable raillery upon himself, that if his name should be known, the ill-natured world might call him "the ass in the lion's skin." This

gentleman's temper is made out of such a happy mixture of the mild and the choleric, that he outdoes both
his predecessors, and has drawn together greater
audiences than have been known in the memory of
man.

I must not conclude my narrative without taking
notice of a groundless report that has been raised to a
gentleman's disadvantage, of whom I must declare
myself an admirer; namely, that Signior Nicolini and
the lion have been seen sitting peaceably by one another,
and smoking a pipe together behind the scenes; by
which their common enemies would insinuate that it is
but a sham combat which they represent upon the
stage: but upon inquiry I find, that if any such corre-
spondence has passed between them, it was not till the
combat was over, when the lion was to be looked upon
as dead according to the received rules of the drama.
Besides, this is what is practised every day in West-
minster Hall, where nothing is more usual than to see
a couple of lawyers, who have been tearing each other
to pieces in the court, embracing one another as soon
as they are out of it.

I would not be thought in any part of this relation
to reflect upon Signior Nicolini, who, in acting this
part, only complies with the wretched taste of his
audience: he knows very well that the lion has many
more admirers than himself; as they say of the famous
equestrian statue on the Pont-Neuf at Paris, that more

people go to see the horse than the king who sits upon it. On the contrary, it gives me a just indignation to see a person whose action gives new majesty to kings, resolution to heroes, and softness to lovers, thus sinking from the greatness of his behaviour, and degraded into the character of the London Prentice. I have often wished that our tragedians would copy after this great master in action. Could they make the same use of their arms and legs, and inform their faces with as significant looks and passions, how glorious would an English tragedy appear with that action which is capable of giving a dignity to the forced thoughts, cold conceits, and unnatural expressions of an Italian opera! In the meantime, I have related this combat of the lion to show what are at present the reigning entertainments of the politer part of Great Britain.

Audiences have often been reproached by writers for the coarseness of their taste; but our present grievance does not seem to be the want of a good taste, but of common sense.

WOMEN AND WIVES.

Parva leves capiunt animos.—
OVID, *Ars Am.*, i. 159.

Light minds are pleased with trifles.

WHEN I was in France, I used to gaze with great
astonishment at the splendid equipages, and party-
coloured habits of that fantastic nation. I was one
day in particular contemplating a lady that sat in a
coach adorned with gilded Cupids, and finely painted
with the Loves of Venus and Adonis. The coach was
drawn by six milk-white horses, and loaden behind
with the same number of powdered footmen. Just
before the lady were a couple of beautiful pages, that
were stuck among the harness, and, by their gay
dresses and smiling features, looked like the elder
brothers of the little boys that were carved and painted
in every corner of the coach.

The lady was the unfortunate Cleanthe, who afterwards gave an occasion to a pretty melancholy novel.
She had for several years received the addresses of a
gentleman, whom, after a long and intimate acquaintance, she forsook upon the account of this shining
equipage, which had been offered to her by one of great
riches but a crazy constitution. The circumstances in
which I saw her were, it seems, the disguises only of

a broken heart, and a kind of pageantry to cover distress, for in two months after, she was carried to her grave with the same pomp and magnificence, being sent thither partly by the loss of one lover and partly by the possession of another.

I have often reflected with myself on this unaccountable humour in womankind, of being smitten with everything that is showy and superficial; and on the numberless evils that befall the sex from this light fantastical disposition. I myself remember a young lady that was very warmly solicited by a couple of importunate rivals, who, for several months together, did all they could to recommend themselves, by complacency of behaviour and agreeableness of conversation. At length, when the competition was doubtful, and the lady undetermined in her choice, one of the young lovers very luckily bethought himself of adding a supernumerary lace to his liveries, which had so good an effect that he married her the very week after.

The usual conversation of ordinary women very much cherishes this natural weakness of being taken with outside and appearance. Talk of a new-married couple, and you immediately hear whether they keep their coach and six, or eat in plate. Mention the name of an absent lady, and it is ten to one but you learn something of her gown and petticoat. A ball is a great help to discourse, and a birthday furnishes conversation

for a twelvemonth after. A furbelow of precious
stones, a hat buttoned with a diamond, a brocade waist-
coat or petticoat, are standing topics. In short, they
consider only the drapery of the species, and never cast
away a thought on those ornaments of the mind that
make persons illustrious in themselves and useful to
others. When women are thus perpetually dazzling
one another's imaginations, and filling their heads with
nothing but colours, it is no wonder that they are more
attentive to the superficial parts of life than the solid
and substantial blessings of it. A girl who has been
trained up in this kind of conversation is in danger of
every embroidered coat that comes in her way. A pair
of fringed gloves may be her ruin. In a word, lace and
ribands, silver and gold galloons, with the like glittering gewgaws, are so many lures to women of weak
minds or low educations, and, when artificially dis-
played, are able to fetch down the most airy coquette
from the wildest of her flights and rambles.

True happiness is of a retired nature, and an enemy
to pomp and noise ; it arises, in the first place, from
the enjoyment of one's self, and, in the next, from the
friendship and conversation of a few select companions;
it loves shade and solitude, and naturally haunts groves
and fountains, fields and meadows ; in short, it feels
everything it wants within itself, and receives no
addition from multitudes of witnesses and spectators.
On the contrary, false happiness loves to be in a

crowd, and to draw the eyes of the world upon her.
She does not receive any satisfaction from the applauses
which she gives herself, but from the admiration she
raises in others. She flourishes in courts and palaces,
theatres and assemblies, and has no existence but when
she is looked upon.

Aurelia, though a woman of great quality, delights
in the privacy of a country life, and passes away a
great part of her time in her own walks and gardens.
Her husband, who is her bosom friend and companion
in her solitudes, has been in love with her ever since
he knew her. They both abound with good sense,
consummate virtue, and a mutual esteem; and are a
perpetual entertainment to one another. Their family
is under so regular an economy, in its hours of devotion
and repast, employment and diversion, that it looks
like a little commonwealth within itself. They often
go into company, that they may return with the greater
delight to one another; and sometimes live in town, not
to enjoy it so properly as to grow weary of it, that they
may renew in themselves the relish of a country life.
By this means they are happy in each other, beloved
by their children, adored by their servants, and are
become the envy, or rather the delight, of all that know
them.

How different to this is the life of Fulvia! She
considers her husband as her steward, and looks upon
discretion and good housewifery as little domestic

virtues unbecoming a woman of quality. She thinks
life lost in her own family, and fancies herself out of
the world when she is not in the ring, the playhouse,
or the drawing-room. She lives in a perpetual motion
of body and restlessness of thought, and is never easy
in any one place when she thinks there is more company in another. The missing of an opera the first
night would be more afflicting to her than the death of
a child. She pities all the valuable part of her own
sex, and calls every woman of a prudent, modest,
retired life, a poor-spirited, unpolished creature. What
a mortification would it be to Fulvia, if she knew that
her setting herself to view is but exposing herself, and
that she grows contemptible by being conspicuous!

I cannot conclude my paper without observing that
Virgil has very finely touched upon this female passion
for dress and show, in the character of Camilla, who,
though she seems to have shaken off all the other weak-
nesses of her sex, is still described as a woman in this
particular. The poet tells us, that after having made a
great slaughter of the enemy, she unfortunately cast
her eye on a Trojan, who wore an embroidered tunic, a
beautiful coat of mail, with a mantle of the finest
purple. "A golden bow," says he, "hung upon his
shoulder; his garment was buckled with a golden
clasp, and his head covered with a helmet of the same
shining metal." The Amazon immediately singled out
this well-dressed warrior, being seized with a woman's

longing for the pretty trappings that he was adorned with :

—*Totumque incauta per agmen,*
Fœmineo prædæ et spoliorum ardebat amore.

.Æn., xi. 781.

—So greedy was she bent
On golden spoils, and on her prey intent.

DRYDEN.

This heedless pursuit after these glittering trifles, the poet, by a nice concealed moral, represents to have been the destruction of his female hero.

— —   ...—

THE ITALIAN OPERA.

—*Equitis quoque jam migravit ab aure voluptas*
Omnis ad incertos oculos, et gaudia vana.

HOR., *Ep.* ii. 1, 187.

But now our nobles too are fops and vain,
Neglect the sense, but love the painted scene.

CREECH.

IT is my design in this paper to deliver down to posterity a faithful account of the Italian opera, and of the gradual progress which it has made upon the English stage ; for there is no question but our great-grandchildren will be very curious to know the reason why their forefathers used to sit together like an audience of foreigners in their own country, and to hear whole plays acted before them in a tongue which they did not understand.

Arsinoë was the first opera that gave us a taste of Italian music. The great success this opera met with produced some attempts of forming pieces upon Italian plans, which should give a more natural and reasonable entertainment than what can be met with in the elaborate trifles of that nation. This alarmed the poetasters and fiddlers of the town, who were used to deal in a more ordinary kind of ware; and therefore laid down an established rule, which is received as such to this day, " That nothing is capable of being well set to music that is not nonsense."

This maxim was no sooner received, but we immediately fell to translating the Italian operas; and as there was no great danger of hurting the sense of those extraordinary pieces, our authors would often make words of their own which were entirely foreign to the meaning of the passages they pretended to translate; their chief care being to make the numbers of the English verse answer to those of the Italian, that both of them might go to the same tune. Thus the famous song in Camilla :

"*Barbara si t' intendo,*" &c.

"Barbarous woman, yes, I know your meaning,".

which expresses the resentments of an angry lover, was translated into that English lamentation,

"Frail are a lover's hopes," &c.

And it was pleasant enough to see the most refined persons of the British nation dying away and languishing to notes that were filled with a spirit of rage and indignation. It happened also very frequently, where the sense was rightly translated, the necessary transposition of words, which were drawn out of the phrase of one tongue into that of another, made the music appear very absurd in one tongue that was very natural in the other. I remember an Italian verse that ran thus, word for word:

"And turned my rage into pity;"

which the English for rhyme's sake translated:

"And into pity turned my rage."

By this means the soft notes that were adapted to pity in the Italian fell upon the word rage in the English; and the angry sounds that were turned to rage in the original, were made to express pity in the translation. It oftentimes happened, likewise, that the finest notes in the air fell upon the most insignificant words in the sentence. I have known the word "and" pursued through the whole gamut; have been entertained with many a melodious "the;" and have heard the most beautiful graces, quavers, and divisions bestowed upon "then," "for," and "from," to the eternal honour of our English particles.

The next step to our refinement was the introducing of Italian actors into our opera; who sang their parts in their own language, at the same time that our countrymen performed theirs in our native tongue. The king or hero of the play generally spoke in Italian, and his slaves answered him in English. The lover frequently made his court, and gained the heart of his princess, in a language which she did not understand. One would have thought it very difficult to have carried on dialogues after this manner without an interpreter between the persons that conversed together; but this was the state of the English stage for about three years.

At length the audience grew tired of understanding half the opera; and therefore, to ease themselves entirely of the fatigue of thinking, have so ordered it at present, that the whole opera is performed in an unknown tongue. We no longer understand the language of our own stage; insomuch that I have often been afraid, when I have seen our Italian performers chattering in the vehemence of action, that they have been calling us names, and abusing us among themselves; but I hope, since we put such an entire confidence in them, they will not talk against us before our faces, though they may do it with the same safety as if it were behind our backs. In the meantime, I cannot forbear thinking how naturally an historian who writes two or three hundred years hence, and does not know the taste of his wise forefathers, will make the following reflection: "In the beginning of the eighteenth century, the Italian tongue was so well understood in England, that operas were acted on the public stage in that language."

One scarce knows how to be serious in the confutation of an absurdity that shows itself at the first sight. It does not want any great measure of sense to see the ridicule of this monstrous practice ; but what makes it the more astonishing, it is not the taste of the rabble, but of persons of the greatest politeness, which has established it.

If the Italians have a genius for music above the English, the English have a genius for other performances of a much higher nature, and capable of giving the mind a much nobler entertainment. Would one think it was possible, at a time when an author lived that was able to write the *Phædra and Hippolitus,* for a people to be so stupidly fond of the Italian opera, as scarce to give a third day's hearing to that admirable tragedy ? Music is certainly a very agreeable entertainment : but if it would take the entire possession of our ears ; if it would make us incapable of hearing sense ; if it would exclude arts that have a much greater tendency to the refinement of human nature ; I must confess I would allow it no better quarter than Plato has done, who banishes it out of his commonwealth.

At present our notions of music are so very uncertain, that we do not know what it is we like ; only, in general, we are transported with anything that is not English: so it be of a foreign growth, let it be Italian, French, or High Dutch, it is the same thing. In short, our English music is quite rooted out, and nothing yet planted in its stead.

When a royal palace is burnt to the ground, every man is at liberty to present his plan for a new one; and, though it be but indifferently put together, it may furnish several hints that may be of use to a good architect. I shall take the same liberty in a following paper of giving my opinion upon the subject of music; which I shall lay down only in a problematical manner, to be considered by those who are masters in the art.

LAMPOONS.

Sævit atrox Volscens, nec teli conspicit usquam
Auctorem, nec quò se ardens immittere possit.

VIRG., *Æn.* ix. 420.

Fierce Volscens foams with rage, and, gazing round,
Descry'd not him who gave the fatal wound;
Nor knew to fix revenge. DRYDEN.

THERE is nothing that more betrays a base, ungenerous spirit than the giving of secret stabs to a man's reputation. Lampoons and satires, that are written with wit and spirit, are like poisoned darts, which not only inflict a wound, but make it incurable. For this reason I am very much troubled when I see the talents of humour and ridicule in the possession of an ill-natured man. There cannot be a greater gratification to a barbarous and inhuman wit, than to stir up sorrow in the heart of a private person, to raise uneasiness among near relations, and to expose whole families to derision, at the same time that he remains unseen and undiscovered. If, besides the accomplishments of being witty and ill-natured, a man is vicious into the bargain, he is one of the most mischievous creatures that can enter into a civil society. His satire will then chiefly fall upon those who ought to be the most exempt from it. Virtue, merit, and everything that is praiseworthy, will be made the subject of ridicule and buffoonery. It is impossible to enumerate the evils which arise from these arrows that fly in the dark; and I know no other excuse that is or can be made for them, than that the wounds they give are only imaginary, and produce nothing more than a secret shame or sorrow in the mind of the suffering person. It must indeed be confessed that a lampoon or a satire do not carry in them robbery or murder; but at the same time, how many are there that would not rather lose a considerable sum of money, or even life itself, than be set up as a mark of infamy and derision? And in this case a man should consider that an injury is not to be measured by the notions of him that gives, but of him that receives it.

Those who can put the best countenance upon the

outrages of this nature which are offered them, are not without their secret anguish. I have often observed a passage in Socrates's behaviour at his death in a light wherein none of the critics have considered it. That excellent man entertaining his friends a little before he drank the bowl of poison, with a discourse on the immortality of the soul, at his entering upon it says that he does not believe any the most comic genius can censure him for talking upon such a subject at such at a time. This passage, I think, evidently glances upon Aristophanes, who writ a comedy on purpose to ridicule the discourses of that divine philosopher. It has been observed by many writers that Socrates was so little moved at this piece of buffoonery, that he was several times present at its being acted upon the stage, and never expressed the least resentment of it. But, with submission, I think the remark I have here made shows us that this unworthy treatment made an impression upon his mind, though he had been too wise to discover it.

When Julius Cæsar was lampooned by Catullus, he invited him to a supper, and treated him with such a generous civility, that he made the poet his friend ever after. Cardinal Mazarine gave the same kind of treatment to the learned Quillet, who had reflected upon his eminence in a famous Latin poem. The cardinal sent for him, and, after some kind expostulations upon what he had written, assured him of his esteem, and dismissed him with a promise of the next good abbey that should fall, which he accordingly conferred upon him in a few months after. This had so good an effect upon the author, that he dedicated the second edition of his book to the cardinal, after having expunged the passages which had given him offence.

Sextus Quintus was not of so generous and forgiving a temper. Upon his being made Pope, the statue of Pasquin was one night dressed in a very dirty shirt, with an excuse written under it, that he was forced to wear foul linen because his laundress was made a princess. This was a reflection upon the Pope's sister, who, before the promotion of her brother, was in those mean circumstances that Pasquin represented her. As this pasquinade made a great noise in Rome, the Pope offered a considerable sum of money to any person that should discover the author of it. The author, relying upon his holiness's generosity, as also on some private overtures which he had received from him, made the discovery himself; upon which the Pope gave him the reward he had promised, but, at the same time, to disable the satirist for the future, ordered his tongue to be cut out, and both his hands to be chopped off. Aretine is too trite an instance. Every one knows that all the kings of Europe were his tributaries. Nay, there is a letter of his extant, in which he makes his boast that he had laid the Sophi of Persia under contribution.

Though in the various examples which I have here drawn together, these several great men behaved themselves very differently towards the wits of the age who had reproached them, they all of them plainly showed that they were very sensible of their reproaches, and consequently that they received them as very great injuries. For my own part, I would never trust a man that I thought was capable of giving these secret wounds; and cannot but think that he would hurt the person, whose reputation he thus assaults, in his body or in his fortune, could he do it with the same security. There is indeed something very barbarous and inhuman in the ordinary scribblers of lampoons. An innocent young lady shall be exposed for an unhappy feature; a father of a family turned to ridicule for some domestic calamity; a wife be made uneasy all her life for a misinterpreted word or action; nay, a good, a temperate, and a just man shall be put out of countenance by the representation of those qualities that should do him honour; so pernicious a thing is wit when it is not tempered with virtue and humanity.

I have indeed heard of heedless, inconsiderate writers that, without any malice, have sacrificed the reputation of their friends and acquaintance to a certain levity of temper, and a silly ambition of distinguishing themselves by a spirit of raillery and satire; as if it were not infinitely more honourable to be a good-natured man than a wit. Where there is this little petulant humour in an author, he is often very mischievous without designing to be so. For which reason I always lay it down as a rule that an indiscreet man is more hurtful than an ill-natured one; for as the one will only attack his enemies, and those he wishes ill to, the other injures indifferently both friends and foes. I cannot forbear, on this occasion, transcribing a fable out of Sir Roger L'Estrange, which accidentally lies before me. A company of waggish boys were watching of frogs at the side of a pond, and still as any of them put up their heads, they would be pelting them down again with stones. "Children," says one of the frogs, "you never consider that though this be play to you, 'tis death to us."

As this week is in a manner set apart and dedicated to serious thoughts, I shall indulge myself in such speculations as may not be altogether unsuitable to the season; and in the meantime, as the settling in ourselves a charitable frame of mind is a work very proper for the time, I have in this paper endeavoured to expose that particular breach of charity which has been generally overlooked by divines, because they are but few who can be guilty of it.

TRUE AND FALSE HUMOUR.

— Risu inepto res ineptior nulla est.
CATULL., *Carm.* 39 *in Egnat.*

Nothing so foolish as the laugh of fools.

AMONG all kinds of writing, there is none in which authors are more apt to miscarry than in works of humour, as there is none in which they are more ambitious to excel. It is not an imagination that teems with monsters, a head that is filled with extravagant conceptions, which is capable of furnishing the world with diversions of this nature; and yet, if we look into the productions of several writers, who set up for men of humour, what wild, irregular fancies, what unnatural distortions of thought do we meet with? If they speak nonsense, they believe they are talking humour; and when they have drawn together a scheme of absurd, inconsistent ideas, they are not able to read it over to themselves without laughing. These poor gentlemen endeavour to gain themselves the reputation of wits and humorists, by such monstrous conceits as almost qualify them for Bedlam; not considering that humour should always lie under the check of reason, and that it requires the direction of the nicest judgment, by so much the more as it indulges itself in the most boundless freedoms. There

is a kind of nature that is to be observed in this sort
of compositions, as well as in all other; and a certain
regularity of thought which must discover the writer
to be a man of sense, at the same time that he appears
altogether given up to caprice. For my part, when I
read the delirious mirth of an unskilful author, I
cannot be so barbarous as to divert myself with it,
but am rather apt to pity the man, than to laugh at
anything he writes.

The deceased Mr. Shadwell, who had himself a great
deal of the talent which I am treating of, represents
an empty rake, in one of his plays, as very much surprised to hear one say that breaking of windows was
not humour; and I question not but several English
readers will be as much startled to hear me affirm,
that many of those raving, incoherent pieces, which are
often spread among us, under odd chimerical titles, are
rather the offsprings of a distempered brain than works
of humour.

It is, indeed, much easier to describe what is not
humour than what is; and very difficult to define it
otherwise than as Cowley has done wit, by negatives.
Were I to give my own notions of it, I would deliver
them after Plato's manner, in a kind of allegory, and,
by supposing Humour to be a person, deduce to him
all his qualifications, according to the following
genealogy. Truth was the founder of the family, and
the father of Good Sense. Good Sense was the father

of Wit, who married a lady of a collateral line called Mirth, by whom he had issue Humour. Humour therefore being the youngest of this illustrious family, and descended from parents of such different dispositions, is very various and unequal in his temper; sometimes you see him putting on grave looks and a solemn habit, sometimes airy in his behaviour and fantastic in his dress; insomuch that at different times he appears as serious as a judge, and as jocular as a merry-andrew. But, as he has a great deal of the mother in his constitution, whatever mood he is in, he never fails to make his company laugh.

But since there is an impostor abroad, who takes upon him the name of this young gentleman, and would willingly pass for him in the world; to the end that well-meaning persons may not be imposed upon by cheats, I would desire my readers, when they meet with this pretender, to look into his parentage, and to examine him strictly, whether or no he be remotely allied to Truth, and lineally descended from Good Sense; if not, they may conclude him a counterfeit. They may likewise distinguish him by a loud and excessive laughter, in which he seldom gets his company to join with him. For as True Humour generally looks serious while everybody laughs about him, False Humour is always laughing whilst everybody about him looks serious. I shall only add, if he has not in him a mixture of both parents—that is, if he would pass for the offspring of Wit without Mirth, or Mirth without Wit, you may conclude him to be altogether spurious and a cheat.

The impostor of whom I am speaking descends originally from Falsehood, who was the mother of Nonsense, who was brought to bed of a son called Phrensy, who married one of the daughters of Folly, commonly known by the name of Laughter, on whom he begot that monstrous infant of which I have been here speaking. I shall set down at length the genealogical table of False Humour, and, at the same time, place under it the genealogy of True Humour, that the reader may at one view behold their different pedigrees and relations :—

Falsehood.

Nonsense.

Phrensy.——Laughter.

False Humour.

Truth.

Good Sense.

Wit.——Mirth,

Humour.

I might extend the allegory, by mentioning several of the children of False Humour, who are more in number than the sands of the sea, and might in particular enumerate the many sons and daughters which he has begot in this island. But as this would be a very invidious task, I shall only observe in general that False Humour differs from the True as a monkey does from a man.

First of all, he is exceedingly given to little apish tricks and buffooneries.

Secondly, he so much delights in mimicry, that it is all one to him whether he exposes by it vice and folly, luxury and avarice; or, on the contrary, virtue and wisdom, pain and poverty.

Thirdly, he is wonderfully unlucky, insomuch that he will bite the hand that feeds him, and endeavour to ridicule both friends and foes indifferently. For, having but small talents, he must be merry where he can, not where he should.

Fourthly, Being entirely void of reason, he pursues no point either of morality or instruction, but is ludicrous only for the sake of being so.

Fifthly, Being incapable of anything but mock representations, his ridicule is always personal, and aimed at the vicious man, or the writer; not at the vice, or at the writing.

I have here only pointed at the whole species of false humorists; but, as one of my principal designs in this paper is to beat down that malignant spirit which discovers itself in the writings of the present age, I shall not scruple, for the future, to single out any of the small wits that infest the world with such compositions as are ill-natured, immoral, and absurd.

This is the only exception which I shall make to the general rule I have prescribed myself, of attacking multitudes; since every honest man ought to look upon himself as in a natural state of war with the libeller and lampooner, and to annoy them wherever they fall in his way. This is but retaliating upon them, and treating them as they treat others.

SA GA YEAN QUA RASH TOW'S IMPRES-SIONS OF LONDON.

Nunquam aliud natura, aliud sapientia dicit.
Juv., *Sat.* xiv. 321.

Good taste and nature always speak the same.

When the four Indian kings were in this country about a twelvemonth ago, I often mixed with the rabble, and followed them a whole day together, being wonderfully struck with the sight of everything that is new or uncommon. I have, since their departure, employed a friend to make many inquiries of their landlord the upholsterer relating to their manners and conversation, as also concerning the remarks which they made in this country; for next to the forming a right notion of such strangers, I should be desirous of learning what ideas they have conceived of us.

The upholsterer finding my friend very inquisitive about these his lodgers, brought him sometime since a little bundle of papers, which he assured him were written by King Sa Ga Yean Qua Rash Tow, and, as he supposes, left behind by some mistake. These papers are now translated, and contain abundance of very odd observations, which I find this little fraternity of kings made during their stay in the Isle of Great Britain. I shall present my reader with a short speci-men of them in this paper, and may perhaps com-municate more to him hereafter. In the article of London are the following words, which without doubt are meant of the church of St. Paul :—

"On the most rising part of the town there stands a huge house, big enough to contain the whole nation of which I am the king. Our good brother E Tow O Koam, King of the Rivers, is of opinion it was made by the hands of that great God to whom it is con-secrated. The Kings of Granajar and of the Six Nations believe that it was created with the earth, and produced on the same day with the sun and moon. But for my own part, by the best information that I could get of this matter, I am apt to think that this prodigious pile was fashioned into the shape it now bears by several tools and instruments, of which they have a wonderful variety in this country. It was probably at first a huge misshapen rock that grew upon the top of the hill, which the natives of the country, after having cut into a kind of regular figure, bored and hollowed with incredible pains and industry, till they had wrought in it all those beautiful vaults and caverns into which it is divided at this day. As soon as this rock was thus curiously scooped to their liking, a prodigious number of hands must have been employed in chipping the outside of it, which is now as smooth as the surface of a pebble; and is in several places hewn out into pillars that stand like the trunks of so many trees bound about the top with garlands of leaves. It is probable that when this great work was begun, which must have been many hundred years ago, there was some religion among this people; for they give it the name of a temple, and have a tradition that it was designed for men to pay their devotion in. And indeed, there are several reasons which make us think that the natives of this country had formerly among them some sort of worship, for they set apart every seventh day as sacred; but upon my going into one of these holy houses on that day, I could not observe any circumstance of devotion in their behaviour. There was, indeed, a man in black, who was mounted above the rest, and seemed to utter something with a great deal of vehemence; but as for those underneath him, instead of paying their worship to the deity of the place, they were most of them bowing and curtsying to one another, and a considerable number of them fast asleep.

" The queen of the country appointed two men to attend us, that had enough of our language to make themselves understood in some few particulars. But we soon perceived these two were great enemies to one another, and did not always agree in the same story. We could make a shift to gather out of one of them that this island was very much infested with a monstrous kind of animals, in the shape of men, called Whigs; and he often told us that he hoped we should meet with none of them in our way, for that, if we did, they would be apt to knock us down for being kings.

" Our other interpreter used to talk very much of a kind of animal called a Tory, that was as great a monster as the Whig, and would treat us as ill for being foreigners. These two creatures, it seems, are born with a secret antipathy to one another, and engage when they meet as naturally as the elephant and the rhinoceros. But as we saw none of either of these species, we are apt to think that our guides deceived us with misrepresentations and fictions, and amused us with an account of such monsters as are not really in their country.

" These particulars we made a shift to pick out from the discourse of our interpreters, which we put together as well as we could, being able to understand but here and there a word of what they said, and afterwards making up the meaning of it among ourselves. The men of the country are very cunning and ingenious in handicraft works, but withal so very idle, that we often saw young, lusty, raw-boned fellows carried up and down the streets in little covered rooms by a couple of porters, who were hired for that service. Their dress is likewise very barbarous, for they almost strangle themselves about the neck, and bind their bodies with many ligatures, that we are apt to think are the occasion of several distempers among them, which our country is entirely free from. Instead of those beautiful feathers with which we adorn our heads, they often buy up a monstrous bush of hair, which covers their heads, and falls down in a large fleece below the middle of their backs. with which they walk up and down the streets, and are as proud of it as if it was of their own growth.

" We were invited to one of their public diversions, where we hoped to have seen the great men of their country running down a stag, or pitching a bar, that we might have discovered who were the persons of the greatest abilities among them; but instead of that, they conveyed us into a huge room lighted up with abundance of candles, where this lazy people sat still above three hours to see several feats of ingenuity performed by others, who it seems were paid for it.

" As for the women of the country, not being able to talk with them, we could only make our remarks upon them at a distance. They let the hair of their heads grow to a great length; but as the men make a great show with heads of hair that are none of their own, the women, who they say have very fine heads of hair, tie it up in a knot, and cover it from being seen. The women look like angels, and would be more beautiful than the sun, were it not for little black spots that are apt to break out in their faces, and sometimes rise in very odd figures. I have observed that those little blemishes wear off very soon; but when they disappear in one part of the face, they are very apt to break out in another, insomuch that I have seen a spot upon the forehead in the afternoon which was upon the chin in the morning."

The author then proceeds to show the absurdity of breeches and petticoats, with many other curious observations, which I shall reserve for another occasion. I cannot, however, conclude this paper without taking notice that amidst these wild remarks there now and then appears something very reasonable. I cannot likewise forbear observing, that we are all guilty in some measure of the same narrow way of thinking which we meet with in this abstract of the Indian journal, when we fancy the customs, dresses, and manners of other countries are ridiculous and extravagant if they do not resemble those of our own.

THE VISION OF MARRATON.

Felices errore suo. —

LUCAN i. 454.

Happy in their mistake.

THE Americans believe that all creatures have souls, not only men and women, but brutes, vegetables, nay, even the most inanimate things, as stocks and stones. They believe the same of all works of art, as of knives, boats, looking-glasses; and that, as any of these things perish, their souls go into another world, which is inhabited by the ghosts of men and women. For this reason they always place by the corpse of their dead friend a bow and arrows, that he may make use of the souls of them in the other world, as he did of their wooden bodies in this. How absurd soever such an opinion as this may appear, our European philosophers have maintained several notions altogether as improbable. Some of Plato's followers, in particular, when they talk of the world of ideas, entertain us with substances and beings no less extravagant and chimerical. Many Aristotelians have likewise spoken as unintelligibly of their substantial forms. I shall only instance Albertus Magnus, who, in his dissertation upon the loadstone, observing that fire will destroy its magnetic virtues, tells us that he took particular notice of one as it lay glowing amidst a heap of burning coals, and that he perceived a certain blue vapour to arise from it, which he believed might be the substantial form that is, in our West Indian phrase, the soul of the loadstone.

There is a tradition among the Americans that one of their countrymen descended in a vision to the great repository of souls, or, as we call it here, to the other world; and that upon his return he gave his friends a distinct account of everything he saw among those regions of the dead. A friend of mine, whom I have formerly mentioned, prevailed upon one of the interpreters of the Indian kings to inquire of them, if possible, what tradition they have among them of this matter: which, as well as he could learn by those many questions which he asked them at several times, was in substance as follows:

The visionary, whose name was Marraton, after having travelled for a long space under a hollow mountain, arrived at length on the confines of this world of spirits, but could not enter it by reason of a thick forest, made up of bushes, brambles, and pointed thorns, so perplexed and interwoven with one another that it was impossible to find a passage through it. Whilst he was looking about for some track or pathway that might be worn in any part of it, he saw a huge lion couched under the side of it, who kept his eye upon him in the same posture as when he watches for his prey. The Indian immediately started back, whilst the lion rose with a spring, and leaped towards him.

Being wholly destitute of all other weapons, he stooped down to take up a huge stone in his hand, but, to his infinite surprise, grasped nothing. and found the supposed stone to be only the apparition of one. If he was disappointed on this side, he was as much pleased on the other, when he found the lion, which had seized on his left shoulder, had no power to hurt him, and was only the ghost of that ravenous creature which it appeared to be. He no sooner got rid of his impotent enemy, but he marched up to the wood, and, after having surveyed it for some time, endeavoured to press into one part of it that was a little thinner than the rest, when, again to his great surprise, he found the bushes made no resistance, but that he walked through briars and brambles with the same ease as through the open air, and, in short, that the whole wood was nothing else but a wood of shades. He immediately concluded that this huge thicket of thorns and brakes was designed as a kind of fence or quickset hedge to the ghosts it inclosed, and that probably their soft substances might be torn by these subtile points and prickles, which were too weak to make any impressions in flesh and blood. With this thought he resolved to travel through this intricate wood, when by degrees he felt a gale of perfumes breathing upon him, that grew stronger and sweeter in proportion as he advanced. He had not proceeded much further, when he observed the thorns and briers to end, and give place to a thousand

beautiful green trees, covered with blossoms of the
finest scents and colours, that formed a wilderness of
sweets, and were a kind of lining to those ragged scenes
which he had before passed through. As he was
coming out of this delightful part of the wood, and
entering upon the plains it enclosed, he saw several
horsemen rushing by him, and a little while after heard
the cry of a pack of dogs. He had not listened long
before he saw the apparition of a milk-white steed,
with a young 'man on the back of it, advancing upon
full stretch after the souls of about a hundred beagles,
that were hunting down the ghost of a hare, which ran
away before them with an unspeakable swiftness. As
the man on the milk-white steed came by him, he looked
upon him very attentively, and found him to be the
young prince Nicharagua, who died about half a year
before, and, by reason of his great virtues, was at that
time lamented over all the western parts of America.

He had no sooner got out of the wood but he was
entertained with such a landscape of flowery plains,
green meadows, running streams, sunny hills, and
shady vales as were not to be represented by his own
expressions, nor, as he said, by the conceptions of
others. This happy region was peopled with innumerable swarms of spirits, who applied themselves to exercises and diversions, according as their fancies led
them. Some of them were tossing the figure of a quoit ;
others were pitching the shadow of a bar ; others were

breaking the apparition of a horse; and multitudes employing themselves upon ingenious handicrafts with the souls of departed utensils, for that is the name which in the Indian language they give their tools when they are burnt or broken. As he travelled through this delightful scene he was very often tempted to pluck the flowers that rose everywhere about him in the greatest variety and profusion, having never seen several of them in his own country: but he quickly found, that though they were objects of his sight, they were not liable to his touch. He at length came to the side of a great river, and, being a good fisherman himself, stood upon the banks of it some time to look upon an angler that had taken a great many shapes of fishes, which lay flouncing up and down by him.

I should have told my reader that this Indian had been formerly married to one of the greatest beauties of his country, by whom he had several children. This couple were so famous for their love and constancy to one another that the Indians to this day, when they give a married man joy of his wife, wish that they may live together like Marraton and Yaratilda. Marraton had not stood long by the fisherman when he saw the shadow of his beloved Yaratilda, who had for some time fixed her eye upon him before he discovered her. Her arms were stretched out towards him; floods of tears ran down her eyes; her looks, her hands, her voice called him over to her, and, at the same time,

seemed to tell him that the river was unpassable. Who
can describe the passion made up of joy, sorrow, love,
desire, astonishment that rose in the Indian upon the
sight of his dear Yaratilda? He could express it by
nothing but his tears, which ran like a river down his
cheeks as he looked upon her. He had not stood in
this posture long before he plunged into the stream that
lay before him, and finding it to be nothing but the
phantom of a river, stalked on the bottom of it till he
arose on the other side. At his approach Yaratilda
flew into his arms, whilst Marraton wished himself
disencumbered of that body which kept her from his
embraces. After many questions and endearments on
both sides, she conducted him to a bower, which she
had dressed with her own hands with all the ornaments that could be met with in those blooming regions.
She had made it gay beyond imagination, and was
every day adding something new to it. As Marraton
stood astonished at the unspeakable beauty of her habi-
tation, and ravished with the fragrancy that came from
every part of it, Yaratilda told him that she was pre-
paring this bower for his reception, as well knowing
that his piety to his God, and his faithful dealing towards men, would certainly bring him to that happy
place whenever his life should be at an end. She then
brought two of her children to him, who died some
years before, and resided with her in the same delightful bower, advising him to breed up those others

which were still with him in such a manner that they might hereafter all of them meet together in this happy place.

The tradition tells us further that he had afterwards a sight of those dismal habitations which are the portion of ill men after death; and mentions several molten seas of gold, in which were plunged the souls of barbarous Europeans, who put to the sword so many thousands of poor Indians for the sake of that precious metal. But having already touched upon the chief points of this tradition, and exceeded the measure of my paper, I shall not give any further account of it.

SIX PAPERS ON WIT.

Ut pictura poësis erit—
HOR., Ars Poet. 361.

Poems like pictures are.

NOTHING is so much admired, and so little understood, as wit. No author that I know of has written professedly upon it. As for those who make any mention of it, they only treat on the subject as it has accidentally fallen in their way, and that too in little short reflections, or in general declamatory flourishes, without entering into the bottom of the matter. I hope, therefore, I shall perform an acceptable work to my countrymen if I treat at large upon this subject; which I shall endeavour to do in a manner suitable to it, that I may not incur the censure which a famous critic bestows upon one who had written a treatise upon " the sublime," in a low grovelling style. I intend to lay aside a whole week for this undertaking, that the scheme of my thoughts may not be broken and interrupted; and I dare promise myself, if my readers will give me a week's attention, that this great city will be very much changed for the better by next Saturday night. I shall endeavour to make what I say intelligible to ordinary capacities; but if my readers meet with any paper that in some parts of it may be a little out of their reach, I would not have them discouraged, for they may assure themselves the next shall be much clearer.

As the great and only end of these my speculations is to banish vice and ignorance out of the territories of Great Britain, I shall endeavour, as much as possible, to establish among us a taste of polite writing. It is with this view that I have endeavoured to set my readers right in several points relating to operas and tragedies, and shall, from time to time, impart my notions of comedy, as I think they may tend to its refinement and perfection. I find by my bookseller, that these papers of criticism, with that upon humour, have met with a more kind reception than indeed I could have hoped for from such subjects; for which reason I shall enter upon my present undertaking with greater cheerfulness.

In this, and one or two following papers, I shall trace out the history of false wit, and distinguish the several kinds of it as they have prevailed in different ages of the world. This I think the more necessary at present, because I observed there were attempts on foot last winter to revive some of those antiquated modes of wit that have been long exploded out of the commonwealth of letters. There were several satires and panegyrics handed about in an acrostic, by which means some of the most arrant undisputed blockheads about the town began to entertain ambitious thoughts, and to set up for polite authors. I shall therefore describe at length those many arts of false wit, in which a writer does not show himself a man of a beautiful genius, but of great industry.

The first species of false wit which I have met with is very venerable for its antiquity, and has produced several pieces which have lived very near as long as the "Iliad" itself: I mean, those short poems printed among the minor Greek poets, which resemble the figure of an egg, a pair of wings, an axe, a shepherd's pipe, and an altar.

As for the first, it is a little oval poem, and may not improperly be called a scholar's egg. I would endeavour to hatch it, or, in more intelligible language, to translate it into English, did not I find the

interpretation of it very difficult; for the author seems
to have been more intent upon the figure of his poem
than upon the sense of it.

The pair of wings consists of twelve verses, or rather
feathers, every verse decreasing gradually in its
measure according to its situation in the wing. The
subject of it, as in the rest of the poems which follow,
bears some remote affinity with the figure, for it
describes a god of love, who is always painted with
wings.

The axe, methinks, would have been a good figure
for a lampoon, had the edge of it consisted of the
most satirical parts of the work; but as it is in the
original, I take it to have been nothing else but the
poesy of an axe which was consecrated to Minerva, and
was thought to be the same that Epeus made use of
in the building of the Trojan horse; which is a hint
I shall leave to the consideration of the critics. I am
apt to think that the poesy was written originally
upon the axe, like those which our modern cutlers
inscribe upon their knives; and that, therefore, the
poesy still remains in its ancient shape, though the
axe itself is lost.

The shepherd's pipe may be said to be full of music,
for it is composed of nine different kinds of verses,
which by their several lengths resemble the nine stops
of the old musical instrument, that is likewise the
subject of the poem.

The altar is inscribed with the epitaph of Troïlus the son of Hecuba; which, by the way, makes me believe that these false pieces of wit are much more ancient than the authors to whom they are generally ascribed; at least, I will never be persuaded that so fine a writer as Theocritus could have been the author of any such simple works.

It was impossible for a man to succeed in these performances who was not a kind of painter, or at least a designer. He was first of all to draw the outline of the subject which he intended to write upon, and afterwards conform the description to the figure of his subject. The poetry was to contract or dilate itself according to the mould in which it was cast. In a word, the verses were to be cramped or extended to the dimensions of the frame that was prepared for them; and to undergo the fate of those persons whom the tyrant Procrustes used to lodge in his iron bed: if they were too short, he stretched them on a rack; and if they were too long, chopped off a part of their legs, till they fitted the couch which he had prepared for them.

Mr. Dryden hints at this obsolete kind of wit in one of the following verses in his "Mac Flecknoe;" which an English reader cannot understand, who does not know that there are those little poems above mentioned in the shape of wings and altars :—

—Choose for thy command
Some peaceful province in acrostic land ;

There may'st thou wings display, and altars raise,
And torture one poor word a thousand ways.

This fashion of false wit was revived by several poets of the last age, and in particular may be met with among Mr. Herbert's poems; and, if I am not mistaken, in the translation of Du Bartas. I do not remember any other kind of work among the moderns which more resembles the performances I have mentioned than that famous picture of King Charles the First, which has the whole Book of Psalms written in the lines of the face, and the hair of the head. When I was last at Oxford I perused one of the whiskers, and was reading the other, but could not go so far in it as I would have done, by reason of the impatience of my friends and fellow-travellers, who all of them pressed to see such a piece of curiosity. I have since heard, that there is now an eminent writing-master in town, who has transcribed all the Old Testament in a full-bottomed periwig: and if the fashion should introduce the thick kind of wigs which were in vogue some few years ago, he promises to add two or three supernumerary locks that should contain all the Apocrypha. He designed this wig originally for King William, having disposed of the two Books of Kings in the two forks of the foretop; but that glorious monarch dying before the wig was finished, there is a space left in it for the face of any one that has a mind to purchase it.

But to return to our ancient poems in picture. I

would humbly propose, for the benefit of our modern smatterers in poetry, that they would imitate their brethren among the ancients in those ingenious devices. I have communicated this thought to a young poetical lover of my acquaintance, who intends to present his mistress with a copy of verses made in the shape of her fan; and, if he tells me true, has already finished the three first sticks of it. He has likewise promised me to get the measure of his mistress's marriage finger with a design to make a posy in the fashion of a ring, which shall exactly fit it. It is so very easy to enlarge upon a good hint, that I do not question but my ingenious readers will apply what I have said to many other particulars; and that we shall see the town filled in a very little time with poetical tippets, handkerchiefs, snuff-boxes, and the like female ornaments. I shall therefore conclude with a word of advice to those admirable English authors who call themselves Pindaric writers, that they would apply themselves to this kind of wit without loss of time, as being provided better than any other poets with verses of all sizes and dimensions.

––––––

Operose nihil agunt.
SENECA.
Busy about nothing.

THERE is nothing more certain than that every man would be a wit if he could; and notwithstanding

pedants of pretended depth and solidity are apt to
decry the writings of a polite author, as flash and
froth, they all of them show, upon occasion, that they
would spare no pains to arrive at the character of those
whom they seem to despise. For this reason we often
find them endeavouring at works of fancy, which cost
them infinite pangs in the production. The truth of it
is, a man had better be a galley-slave than a wit, were
one to gain that title by those elaborate trifles which
have been the inventions of such authors as were often
masters of great learning, but no genius.

In my last paper I mentioned some of these false
wits among the ancients; and in this shall give the
reader two or three other species of them, that flourished
in the same early ages of the world. The first I shall
produce are the lipogrammatists or letter-droppers of
antiquity, that would take an exception, without any
reason, against some particular letter in the alphabet,
so as not to admit it once into a whole poem. One
Tryphiodorus was a great master in this kind of
writing. He composed an "Odyssey" or epic poem
on the adventures of Ulysses, consisting of four-and-
twenty books, having entirely banished the letter A
from his first book, which was called Alpha, as *lucus à
non lucendo*, because there was not an Alpha in it.
His second book was inscribed Beta for the same
reason. In short, the poet excluded the whole four-
and-twenty letters in their turns, and showed them,

one after another, that he could do his business without them.

It must have been very pleasant to have seen this poet avoiding the reprobate letter, as much as another would a false quantity, and making his escape from it through the several Greek dialects, when he was pressed with it in any particular syllable. For the most apt and elegant word in the whole language was rejected, like a diamond with a flaw in it, if it appeared blemished with a wrong letter. I shall only observe upon this head, that if the work I have here mentioned had been now extant, the "Odyssey" of Tryphiodorus, in all probability, would have been oftener quoted by our learned pedants than the "Odyssey" of Homer. What a perpetual fund would it have been of obsolete words and phrases, unusual barbarisms and rusticities, absurd spellings and complicated dialects! I make no question but that it would have been looked upon as one of the most valuable treasuries of the Greek tongue.

I find likewise among the ancients that ingenious kind of conceit which the moderns distinguish by the name of a rebus, that does not sink a letter, but a whole word, by substituting a picture in its place. When Cæsar was one of the masters of the Roman mint, he placed the figure of an elephant upon the reverse of the public money; the word Cæsar signifying an elephant in the Punic language. This was artificially contrived by Cæsar, because it was not lawful for a private man to stamp his own figure upon the coin of the commonwealth. Cicero, who was so called from the founder of his family, that was marked on the nose with a little wen like a vetch, which is *Cicer* in Latin, instead of Marcus Tullius Cicero, ordered the words Marcus Tullius, with a figure of a vetch at the end of them, to be inscribed on a public monument. This was done probably to show that he was neither ashamed of his name nor family, notwithstanding the envy of his competitors had often reproached him with both. In the same manner we read of a famous building that was marked in several parts of it with the figures of a frog and a lizard; those words in Greek having been the names of the architects, who by the laws of their country were never permitted to inscribe their own names upon their works. For the same reason it is thought that the forelock of the horse, in the antique equestrian statue of Marcus Aurelius, represents at a distance the shape of an owl, to intimate the country of the statuary, who, in all probability, was an Athenian. This kind of wit was very much in vogue among our own countrymen about an age or two ago, who did not practise it for any oblique reason, as the ancients above-mentioned, but purely for the sake of being witty. Among innumerable instances that may be given of this nature, I shall produce the device of one Mr. Newberry, as I find it mentioned by our learned Camden in his Remains. Mr. Newberry, to represent his name by a picture, hung up at his door the sign of a yew-tree, that has several berries upon it, and in the midst of them a great golden N hung upon a bough of the tree, which by the help of a little false spelling made up the word N-ew-berry.

I shall conclude this topic with a rebus, which has been lately hewn out in freestone, and erected over two of the portals of Blenheim House, being the figure of a monstrous lion tearing to pieces a little cock. For the better understanding of which device I must acquaint my English reader that a cock has the misfortune to be called in Latin by the same word that signifies a Frenchman, as a lion is the emblem of the English nation. Such a device in so noble a pile of building looks like a pun in an heroic poem; and I am very sorry the truly ingenious architect would suffer the statuary to blemish his excellent plan with so poor a conceit. But I hope what I have said will gain quarter for the cock, and deliver him out of the lion's paw.

I find likewise in ancient times the conceit of making an echo talk sensibly, and give rational answers. If this could be excusable in any writer, it would be in Ovid where he introduces the Echo as a nymph, before she was worn away into nothing but a voice. The learned Erasmus, though a man of wit and genius, has composed a dialogue upon this silly kind of device, and

made use of an Echo, who seems to have been a very
extraordinary linguist, for she answers the person she
talks with in Latin, Greek, and Hebrew, according as
she found the syllables which she was to repeat in any
of those learned languages. Hudibras, in ridicule of
this false kind of wit, has described Bruin bewailing
the loss of his bear to the solitary Echo, who is of great
use to the poet in several distiches, as she does not only
repeat after him, but helps out his verse, and furnishes
him with rhymes :—

> He raged, and kept as heavy a coil as
> Stout Hercules for loss of Hylas ;
> Forcing the valleys to repeat
> The accents of his sad regret ;
> He beat his breast, and tore his hair,
> For loss of his dear crony bear :
> That Echo from the hollow ground
> His doleful wailings did resound
> More wistfully by many times,
> Than in small poets' splay-foot rhymes,
> That make her, in their rueful stories,
> To answer to int'rogatories,
> And most unconscionably depose
> Things of which she nothing knows ;
> And when she has said all she can say,
> 'Tis wrested to the lover's fancy.
> Quoth he, "O whither, wicked Bruin,
> Art thou fled to my "——Echo, *Ruin ?*
> "I thought th' hadst scorn'd to budge a step
> For fear." Quoth Echo, *Marry guep.*
> "Am I not here to take thy part?"
> Then what has quell'd thy stubborn heart ?
> Have these bones rattled, and this head

So often in thy quarrel bled?
Nor did I ever winch or grudge it,
For thy dear sake." Quoth she, *Mum budget*.
Think'st thou 'twill not be laid i' th' dish,
Thou turn'dst thy back?" Quoth Echo, *Pish*.
To run from those th' hadst overcome
Thus cowardly?" Quoth Echo, *Mum*.
" But what a-vengeance makes thee fly
From me too as thine enemy?
Or if thou hadst no thought of me,
Nor what I have endured for thee,
Yet shame and honour might prevail
To keep thee thus from turning tail:
For who would grudge to spend his blood in
His honour's cause?" Quoth she, *A pudding*.

Part I., *Cant.* 3, 183.

Hoc est quod palles? Cur quis non prandeat, hoc est?
PERS., *Sa'.* iii. 85.

Is it for this you gain those meagre looks,
And sacrifice your dinner to your books?

SEVERAL kinds of false wit that vanished in the refined ages of the world, discovered themselves again in
the times of monkish ignorance.

As the monks were the masters of all that little
learning which was then extant, and had their whole
lives entirely disengaged from business, it is no wonder
that several of them, who wanted genius for higher
performances, employed many hours in the composition
of such tricks in writing as required much time and
little capacity. I have seen half the " Æneid " turned

into Latin rhymes by one of the *beaux esprits* of that
dark age: who says, in his preface to it, that the
" Æneid " wanted nothing but the sweets of rhyme to
make it the most perfect work in its kind. I have likewise seen a hymn in hexameters to the Virgin Mary,
which filled a whole book, though it consisted but of the
eight following words :—

Tot tibi sunt, Virgo, dotes, quot sidera cœlo.

Thou hast as many virtues, O Virgin, as there are stars in
heaven.

The poet rang the changes upon these eight several
words, and by that means made his verses almost as
numerous as the virtues and stars which they celebrated.
It is no wonder that men who had so much time upon
their hands did not only restore all the antiquated
pieces of false wit, but enriched the world with inventions of their own. It is to this age that we owe
the production of anagrams, which is nothing else but
a transmutation of one word into another, or the turning of the same set of letters into different words;
which may change night into day, or black into white,
if chance, who is the goddess that presides over these
sorts of composition, shall so direct. I remember a
witty author, in allusion to this kind of writing, calls
his rival, who, it seems, was distorted, and had his
limbs set in places that did not properly belong to
them, " the anagram of a man."

When the anagrammatist takes a name to work upon, he considers it at first as a mine not broken up, which will not show the treasure it contains till he shall have spent many hours in the search of it; for it is his business to find out one word that conceals itself in another, and to examine the letters in all the variety of stations in which they can possibly be ranged. I have heard of a gentleman who, when this kind of wit was in fashion, endeavoured to gain his mistress's heart by it. She was one of the finest women of her age, and known by the name of the Lady Mary Boon. The lover not being able to make anything of Mary, by certain liberties indulged to this kind of writing converted it into Moll; and after having shut himself up for half a year, with indefatigable industry produced an anagram. Upon the presenting it to his mistress, who was a little vexed in her heart to see herself degraded into Moll Boon, she told him, to his infinite surprise, that he had mistaken her surname, for that it was not Boon, but Bohun.

— *Ibi omnis*
Effusus labor.—

The lover was thunder-struck with his misfortune, insomuch that in a little time after he lost his senses, which, indeed, had been very much impaired by that continual application he had given to his anagram.

The acrostic was probably invented about the same time with the anagram, though it is impossible to decide whether the inventor of the one or the other were the greater blockhead. The simple acrostic is nothing but the name or title of a person, or thing, made out of the initial letters of several verses, and by that means written, after the manner of the Chinese, in a perpendicular line. But besides these there are compound acrostics, when the principal letters stand two or three deep. I have seen some of them where the verses have not only been edged by a name at each extremity, but have had the same name running down like a seam through the middle of the poem.

There is another near relation of the anagrams and acrostics, which is commonly called a chronogram. This kind of wit appears very often on many modern medals, especially those of Germany, when they represent in the inscription the year in which they were coined. Thus we see on a medal of Gustavus Adolphus the following words, CHRIsTVs DuX ERGO TRIVMPHVs. If you take the pains to pick the figures out of the several words, and range them in their proper order, you will find they amount to MDCXVVVII, or 1627, the year in which the medal was stamped: for as some of the letters distinguish themselves from the rest, and overtop their fellows, they are to be considered in a double capacity, both as letters and as figures. Your laborious German wits will turn over a whole dictionary for one of these ingenious devices. A man would think they were searching after an apt classical term, but instead of that they are looking out a word that has an L, an M, or a D in it. When, therefore, we meet with any of these inscriptions, we are not so much to look in them for the thought, as for the year of the Lord.

The *bouts-rimés* were the favourites of the French nation for a whole age together, and that at a time when it abounded in wit and learning. They were a list of words that rhyme to one another, drawn up by another hand, and given to a poet, who was to make a poem to the rhymes in the same order that they were placed upon the list: the more uncommon the rhymes were, the more extraordinary was the genius of the poet that could accommodate his verses to them. I do not know any greater instance of the decay of wit and learning among the French, which generally follows the declension of empire, than the endeavouring to restore this foolish kind of wit. If the reader will be at trouble to see examples of it, let him look into the new *Mercure Gallant*, where the author every month gives a list of rhymes to be filled up by the ingenious, in order to be communicated to the public in the *Mercure* for the succeeding month. That for the month of November last, which now lies before me, is as follows :—

. . . . Lauriers
. . . . Guerriers

. . . . Musette
. . . . Lisette

. . . . Cæsars
. . . . Etendars
. . . . Houlette
. . . . Foletto

One would be amazed to see so learned a man as
Menage talking seriously on this kind of trifle in the
following passage :—

"Monsieur de la Chambre has told me that he never
knew what he was going to write when he took his
pen into his hand; but that one sentence always produced another. For my own part, I never knew what
I should write next when I was making verses. In
the first place I got all my rhymes together, and was
afterwards perhaps three or four months in filling
them up. I one day showed Monsieur Gombaud a
composition of this nature, in which, among others, I
had made use of the four following rhymes, Amaryllis,
Phyllis, Marne, Arne; desiring him to give me his
opinion of it. He told me immediately that my
verses were good for nothing. And upon my asking
his reason, he said, because the rhymes are too common,
and for that reason easy to be put into verse. 'Marry,'
says I, 'if it be so, I am very well rewarded for all
the pains I have been at!' But by Monsieur Gombaud's
leave, notwithstanding the severity of the criticism,

the verses were good." (*Vide* "Menagiana.") Thus far the learned Menage, whom I have translated word for word.

The first occasion of these *bouts-rimés* made them in some manner excusable, as they were tasks which the French ladies used to impose on their lovers. But when a grave author, like him above-mentioned, tasked himself, could there be anything more ridiculous? Or would not one be apt to believe that the author played booty, and did not make his list of rhymes till he had finished his poem?

I shall only add that this piece of false wit has been finely ridiculed by Monsieur Sarasin, in a poem entitled "La Défaite des Bouts-Rimés" (The Rout of the Bouts-Rimés).

I must subjoin to this last kind of wit the double rhymes, which are used in doggrel poetry, and generally applauded by ignorant readers. If the thought of the couplet in such compositions is good, the rhyme adds little to it; and if bad, it will not be in the power of the rhyme to recommend it. I am afraid that great numbers of those who admire the incomparable "Hudibras," do it more on account of these doggrel rhymes than of the parts that really deserve admiration. I am sure I have heard the

> Pulpit, drum ecclesiastic,
> Was beat with fist, instead of a stick (*Canto* 1, 11),

and—

There was an ancient philosopher
Who had read Alexander Ross over (*Part I., Canto* 2, 1),

more frequently quoted than the finest pieces of wit
in the whole poem.

Non equidem hoc studeo bullatis ut mihi nugis
Pagina turgescat, dare pondus idonea fumo.

PERS., *Sat.* v. 19.

'Tis not indeed my talent to engage
In lofty trifles, or to swell my page
With wind and noise.   DRYDEN.

THERE is no kind of false wit which has been so
recommended by the practice of all ages as that which
consists in a jingle of words, and is comprehended
under the general name of punning. It is indeed impossible to kill a weed which the soil has a natural
disposition to produce. The seeds of punning are in
the minds of all men, and though they may be subdued
by reason, reflection, and good sense, they will be very
apt to shoot up in the greatest genius that is not broken
and cultivated by the rules of art. Imitation is natural
to us, and when it does not raise the mind to poetry,
painting, music, or other more noble arts, it often
breaks out in puns and quibbles.

Aristotle, in the eleventh chapter of his book of
rhetoric, describes two or three kinds of puns, which
he calls paragrams, among the beauties of good

writing, and produces instances of them out of some of
the greatest authors in the Greek tongue. Cicero has
sprinkled several of his works with puns, and, in his
book where he lays down the rules of oratory, quotes
abundance of sayings as pieces of wit, which also,
upon examination, prove arrant puns. But the age in
which the pun chiefly flourished was in the reign of
King James the First. That learned monarch was
himself a tolerable punster, and made very few bishops
or Privy Councillors that had not some time or other
signalised themselves by a clinch, or a conundrum. It
was, therefore, in this age that the pun appeared with
pomp and dignity. It had been before admitted into
merry speeches and ludicrous compositions, but was
now delivered with great gravity from the pulpit, or
pronounced in the most solemn manner at the council-
table. The greatest authors, in their most serious
works, made frequent use of puns. The sermons of
Bishop Andrews, and the tragedies of Shakespeare,
are full of them. The sinner was punned into repent-
ance by the former; as in the latter, nothing is more
usual than to see a hero weeping and quibbling for a
dozen lines together.

I must add to these great authorities, which seem to
have given a kind of sanction to this piece of false wit,
that all the writers of rhetoric have treated of punning with very great respect, and divided the several
kinds of it into hard names, that are reckoned among

the figures of speech, and recommended as ornaments in discourse. I remember a country schoolmaster of my acquaintance told me once, that he had been in company with a gentleman whom he looked upon to be the greatest paragrammatist among the moderns. Upon inquiry, I found my learned friend had dined that day with Mr. Swan, the famous punster; and desiring him to give me some account of Mr. Swan's conversation, he told me that he generally talked in the *Paranomasia*, that he sometimes gave in to the *Plocé*, but that in his humble opinion he shone most in the *Antanaclasis*.

I must not here omit that a famous university of this land was formerly very much infested with puns; but whether or not this might arise from the fens and marshes in which it was situated, and which are now drained, I must leave to the determination of more skilful naturalists.

After this short history of punning, one would wonder how it should be so entirely banished out of the learned world as it is at present, especially since it had found a place in the writings of the most ancient polite authors. To account for this we must consider that the first race of authors, who were the great heroes in writing, were destitute of all rules and arts of criticism; and for that reason, though they excel later writers in greatness of genius, they fall short of them in accuracy and correctness. The moderns cannot reach their beauties, but can avoid their imperfections. When the world was furnished with these authors of the first eminence, there grew up another set of writers, who gained themselves a reputation by the remarks which they made on the works of those who preceded them. It was one of the employments of these secondary authors to distinguish the several kinds of wit by terms of art, and to consider them as more or less perfect, according as they were founded in truth. It is no wonder, therefore, that even such authors as Isocrates, Plato, and Cicero, should have such little blemishes as are not to be met with in authors of a much inferior character, who have written since those several blemishes were discovered. I do not find that there was a proper separation made between puns and true wit by any of the ancient authors, except Quintilian and Longinus. But when this distinction was once settled, it was very natural for all men of sense to agree in it. As for the revival of this false wit, it happened about the time of the revival of letters; but as soon as it was once detected, it immediately vanished and disappeared. At the same time there is no question but, as it has sunk in one age and rose in another, it will again recover itself in some distant period of time, as pedantry and ignorance shall prevail upon wit and sense. And, to speak the truth, I do very much apprehend, by some of the last winter's productions, which had their sets of admirers, that our posterity will in a few years degenerate into a race of punsters: at least, a man may be very excusable for any apprehensions of this kind, that has seen acrostics handed about the town with great secresy and applause; to which I must also add a little epigram called the "Witches' Prayer," that fell into verse when it was read either backward or forward, excepting only that it cursed one way, and blessed the other. When one sees there are actually such painstakers among our British wits, who can tell what it may end in? If we must lash one another, let it be with the manly strokes of wit and satire: for I am of the old philosopher's opinion, that, if I must suffer from one or the other, I would rather it should be from the paw of a lion than from the hoof of an ass. I do not speak this out of any spirit of party. There is a most crying dulness on both sides. I have seen Tory acrostics and Whig anagrams, and do not quarrel with either of them because they are Whigs or Tories, but because they are anagrams and acrostics.

But to return to punning. Having pursued the history of a pun, from its original to its downfall, I shall here define it to be a conceit arising from the use of two words that agree in the sound, but differ in the sense. The only way, therefore, to try a piece of wit is to translate it into a different language. If it bears the test, you may pronounce it true; but if it vanishes in the experiment, you may conclude it to

have been a pun. In short, one may say of a pun, as
the countryman described his nightingale, that it is
" *vox et præterea nihil*"—" a sound, and nothing but a
sound." On the contrary, one may represent true wit .
by the description which Aristænetus makes of a fine
woman :—" When she is dressed she is beautiful : when
she is undressed she is beautiful; " or, as Mercerus
has translated it more emphatically, *Induitur, formosa
est : exuitur, ipsa forma est.*

Scribendi recte sapere est et principium, et fons.

HOR., *Ars Poet.* 309.

Sound judgment is the ground of writing well.—ROSCOMMON.

MR. LOCKE has an admirable reflection upon the
difference of wit and judgment, whereby he endeavours
to show the reason why they are not always the talents
of the same person. His words are as follow :—" And
hence, perhaps, may be given some reason of that common observation, ' That men who have a great deal of
wit, and prompt memories, have not always the clearest
judgment or deepest reason.' For wit lying most in
the assemblage of ideas, and putting those together
with quickness and variety wherein can be found any
resemblance or congruity, thereby to make up pleasant
pictures and agreeable visions in the fancy : judgment,

on the contrary, lies quite on the other side, in separating carefully one from another, ideas wherein can be found the least difference, thereby to avoid being misled by similitude, and by affinity to take one thing for another. This is a way of proceeding quite contrary to metaphor and allusion, wherein, for the most part, lies that entertainment and pleasantry of wit which strikes so lively on the fancy, and is therefore so acceptable to all people."

This is, I think, the best and most philosophical account that I have ever met with of wit, which generally, though not always, consists in such a resemblance and congruity of ideas as this author mentions. I shall only add to it, by way of explanation, that every resemblance of ideas is not that which we call wit, unless it be such an one that gives delight and surprise to the reader. These two properties seem essential to wit, more particularly the last of them. In order, therefore, that the resemblance in the ideas be wit, it is necessary that the ideas should not lie too near one another in the nature of things; for, where the likeness is obvious, it gives no surprise. To compare one man's singing to that of another, or to represent the whiteness of any object by that of milk and snow, or the variety of its colours by those of the rainbow, cannot be called wit, unless, besides this obvious resemblance, there be some further congruity discovered in the two ideas that is capable of giving the reader some surprise.

Thus, when a poet tells us the bosom of his mistress is as white as snow, there is no wit in the comparison; but when he adds, with a sigh, it is as cold too, it then grows into wit. Every reader's memory may supply him with innumerable instances of the same nature. For this reason, the similitudes in heroic poets, who endeavour rather to fill the mind with great conceptions than to divert it with such as are new and surprising, have seldom anything in them that can be called wit. Mr. Locke's account of wit, with this short explanation, comprehends most of the species of wit, as metaphors, similitudes, allegories, enigmas, mottoes, parables, fables, dreams, visions, dramatic writings, burlesque, and all the methods of allusion : as there are many other pieces of wit, how remote soever they may appear at first sight from the foregoing description, which upon examination will be found to agree with it.

As true wit generally consists in this resemblance and congruity of ideas, false wit chiefly consists in the resemblance and congruity sometimes of single letters, as in anagrams, chronograms, lipograms, and acrostics; sometimes of syllables, as in echoes and doggrel rhymes ; sometimes of words, as in puns and quibbles ; and sometimes of whole sentences or poems, cast into the figures of eggs, axes, or altars; nay, some carry the notion of wit so far as to ascribe it even to external mimicry, and to look upon a man as an ingenious person that can resemble the tone, posture, or face of another.

As true wit consists in the resemblance of ideas, and false wit in the resemblance of words, according to the foregoing instances, there is another kind of wit which consists partly in the resemblance of ideas and partly in the resemblance of words, which for distinction sake I shall call mixed wit. This kind of wit is that which abounds in Cowley more than in any author that ever wrote. Mr. Waller has likewise a great deal of it. Mr. Dryden is very sparing in it. Milton had a genius much above it. Spenser is in the same class with Milton. The Italians, even in their epic poetry, are full of it. Monsieur Boileau, who formed himself upon the ancient poets, has everywhere rejected it with scorn. If we look after mixed wit among the Greek writers, we shall find it nowhere but in the epigrammatists. There are indeed some strokes of it in the little poem ascribed to Musæus, which by that as well as many other marks betrays itself to be a modern composition. If we look into the Latin writers we find none of this mixed wit in Virgil, Lucretius, or Catullus; very little in Horace, but a great deal of it in Ovid, and scarce anything else in Martial.

Out of the innumerable branches of mixed wit, I shall choose one instance which may be met with in all the writers of this class. The passion of love in its nature has been thought to resemble fire, for which

reason the words "fire" and "flame" are made use of
to signify love. The witty poets, therefore, have taken
an advantage, from the doubtful meaning of the word
"fire." to make an infinite number of witticisms. Cowley observing the cold regard of his mistress's eyes, and
at the same time the power of producing love in him,
considers them as burning-glasses made of ice; and,
finding himself able to live in the greatest extremities
of love, concludes the torrid zone to be habitable.
When his mistress has read his letter written in juice
of lemon, by holding it to the fire, he desires her to
read it over a second time by love's flames. When she
weeps, he wishes it were inward heat that distilled
those drops from the limbec. When she is absent, he
is beyond eighty, that is, thirty degrees nearer the pole
than when she is with him. His ambitious love is a
fire that naturally mounts upwards; his happy love is
the beams of heaven, and his unhappy love flames of
hell. When it does not let him sleep, it is a flame
that sends up no smoke; when it is opposed by counsel
and advice, it is a fire that rages the more by the
winds blowing upon it. Upon the dying of a tree, in
which he had cut his loves, he observes that his
written flames had burnt up and withered the tree.
When he resolves to give over his passion, he tells us
that one burnt like him for ever dreads the fire. His
heart is an Ætna, that, instead of Vulcan's shop,
encloses Cupid's forge in it. His endeavouring to

drown his love in wine is throwing oil upon the fire.
He would insinuate to his mistress that the fire of love,
like that of the sun, which produces so many living
creatures, should not only warm, but beget. Love in
another place cooks Pleasure at his fire. Sometimes the
poet's heart is frozen in every breast, and sometimes
scorched in every eye. Sometimes he is drowned in
tears and burnt in love, like a ship set on fire in the
middle of the sea.

The reader may observe in every one of these instances that the poet mixes the qualities of fire with
those of love; and in the same sentence, speaking of
it both as a passion and as real fire, surprises the reader
with those seeming resemblances or contradictions that
make up all the wit in this kind of writing. Mixed
wit, therefore, is a composition of pun and true wit,
and is more or less perfect as the resemblance lies in
the ideas or in the words. Its foundations are laid
partly in falsehood and partly in truth; reason puts in
her claim for one half of it, and extravagance for the
other. The only province, therefore, for this kind of
wit is epigram, or those little occasional poems that
in their own nature are nothing else but a tissue of
epigrams. I cannot conclude this head of mixed wit
without owning that the admirable poet, out of whom
I have taken the examples of it, had as much true wit
as any author that ever wrote; and indeed all other
talents of an extraordinary genius.

It may be expected, since I am upon this subject, that I should take notice of Mr. Dryden's definition of wit, which, with all the deference that is due to the judgment of so great a man, is not so properly a definition of wit as of good writing in general. Wit, as he defines it, is "a propriety of words and thoughts adapted to the subject." If this be a true definition of wit, I am apt to think that Euclid was the greatest wit that ever set pen to paper. It is certain there never was a greater propriety of words and thoughts adapted to the subject than what that author has made use of in his Elements. I shall only appeal to my reader if this definition agrees with any notion he has of wit. If it be a true one, I am sure Mr. Dryden was not only a better poet, but a greater wit than Mr. Cowley, and Virgil a much more facetious man than either Ovid or Martial.

Bouhours, whom I look upon to be the most penetrating of all the French critics, has taken pains to show that it is impossible for any thought to be beautiful which is not just, and has not its foundation in the nature of things; that the basis of all wit is truth; and that no thought can be valuable of which good sense is not the groundwork. Boileau has endeavoured to inculcate the same notion in several parts of his writings, both in prose and verse. This is that natural way of writing, that beautiful simplicity which we so much admire in the compositions of the ancients, and which nobody deviates from but those who want strength of genius to make a thought shine in its own natural beauties. Poets who want this strength of genius to give that majestic simplicity to nature, which we so much admire in the works of the ancients, are forced to hunt after foreign ornaments, and not to let any piece of wit of what kind soever escape them. I look upon these writers as Goths in poetry, who, like those in architecture, not being able to come up to the beautiful simplicity of the old Greeks and Romans, have endeavoured to supply its place with all the extravagancies of an irregular fancy. Mr. Dryden makes a very handsome observation on Ovid's writing a letter from Dido to Æneas, in the following words: "Ovid," says he, speaking of Virgil's fiction of Dido and Æneas, "takes it up after him, even in the same age, and makes an ancient heroine of Virgil's new-created Dido; dictates a letter for her just before her death to the ungrateful fugitive, and, very unluckily for him- self, is for measuring a sword with a man so much superior in force to him on the same subject. I think I may be judge of this, because I have translated both. The famous author of ' The Art of Love ' has nothing of his own; he borrows all from a greater master in his own profession, and, which is worse, improves nothing which he finds. Nature fails him; and, being forced to his old shift, he has recourse to witticism. This passes indeed with his soft ad-

mirers, and gives him the preference to Virgil in their
esteem."

Were not I supported by so great an authority as that
of Mr. Dryden. I should not venture to observe that the
taste of most of our English poets, as well as readers,
is extremely Gothic. He quotes Monsieur Segrais for
a threefold distinction of the readers of poetry; in the
first of which he comprehends the rabble of readers,
whom he does not treat as such with regard to their
quality, but to their numbers and the coarseness of
their taste. His words are as follows : " Segrais has
distinguished the readers of poetry, according to their
capacity of judging, into three classes." [He might
have said the same of writers too if he had pleased.]
"In the lowest form he places those whom he calls
Les Petits Esprits, such things as our upper-gallery
audience in a playhouse, who like nothing but the
husk and rind of wit, and prefer a quibble, a conceit,
an epigram, before solid sense and elegant expression.
These are mob readers. If Virgil and Martial stood
for Parliament-men, we know already who would carry
it. But though they made the greatest appearance in
the field, and cried the loudest, the best of it is they
are but a sort of French Huguenots, or Dutch boors,
brought over in herds, but not naturalised : who have
not lands of two pounds per annum in Parnassus,
and therefore are not privileged to poll. Their authors
are of the same level, fit to represent them on a

mountebank's stage, or to be masters of the ceremonies in a bear-garden; yet these are they who have the most admirers. But it often happens, to their mortification, that as their readers improve their stock of sense, as they may by reading better books, and by conversation with men of judgment, they soon forsake them."

I must not dismiss this subject without observing that, as Mr. Locke, in the passage above-mentioned, has discovered the most fruitful source of wit, so there is another of a quite contrary nature to it, which does likewise branch itself into several kinds. For not only the resemblance, but the opposition of ideas does very often produce wit, as I could show in several little points, turns, and antitheses that I may possibly enlarge upon in some future speculation.

Humano capiti cervicem pictor equinam
Jungere si velit, et varias inducere plumas,
Undique collatis membris, ut turpiter atrum
Desinat in piscem mulier formosa superne ;
Spectatum admissi risum teneatis, amici ?
Credite, Pisones, isti tabulae, fore librum
Persimilem, cujus, velut aegri somnia, vanae
Fingentur species.

HOR., *Ars Poet.* 1.

If in a picture, Piso, you should see
A handsome woman with a fish's tail,

Or a man's head upon a horse's neck,
Or limbs of beasts, of the most different kinds,
Cover'd with feathers of all sorts of birds,—
Would you not laugh, and think the painter mad?
Trust me, that book is as ridiculous
Whose incoherent style, like sick men's dreams,
Varies all shapes, and mixes all extremes.

ROSCOMMON.

IT is very hard for the mind to disengage itself from a subject in which it has been long employed. The thoughts will be rising of themselves from time to time, though we give them no encouragement: as the tossings and fluctuations of the sea continue several hours after the winds are laid.

It is to this that I impute my last night's dream or vision, which formed into one continued allegory the several schemes of wit, whether false, mixed, or true, that have been the subject of my late papers.

Methought I was transported into a country that was filled with prodigies and enchantments, governed by the goddess of Falsehood, and entitled the Region of False Wit. There was nothing in the fields, the woods, and the rivers, that appeared natural. Several of the trees blossomed in leaf-gold, some of them produced bone-lace, and some of them precious stones. The fountains bubbled in an opera tune, and were filled with stags, wild boars, and mermaids, that lived among the waters; at the same time that dolphins and several kinds of fish played upon the banks, or took their pastime in the meadows. The birds had many of them golden beaks, and human voices. The flowers perfumed the air with smells of incense, ambergris, and pulvillios; and were so interwoven with one another, that they grew up in pieces of embroidery. The winds were filled with sighs and messages of distant lovers. As I was walking to and fro in this enchanted wilderness, I could not forbear breaking out into soliloquies upon the several wonders which lay before me, when, to my great surprise, I found there were artificial echoes in every walk, that, by repetitions of certain words which I spoke, agreed with me or contradicted me in everything I said. In the midst of my conversation with these invisible companions, I discovered in the centre of a very dark grove a monstrous fabric built after the Gothic manner, and covered with innumerable devices in that barbarous kind of sculpture. I immediately went up to it, and found it to be a kind of heathen temple consecrated to the god of Dulness. Upon my entrance I saw the deity of the place, dressed in the habit of a monk, with a book in one hand and a rattle in the other. Upon his right hand was Industry, with a lamp burning before her; and on his left, Caprice, with a monkey sitting on her shoulder. Before his feet there stood an altar of a very odd make, which, as I afterwards found, was shaped in that manner to comply with the inscription that surrounded it. Upon the altar there lay several offerings of axes, wings, and eggs, cut in paper, and inscribed with verses. The temple was filled with votaries, who applied themselves to different diversions, as their fancies directed them. In one part of it I saw a regiment of anagrams, who were continually in motion, turning to the right or to the left, facing about, doubling their ranks, shifting their stations, and throwing themselves into all the figures and counter-marches of the most changeable and perplexed exercise.

Not far from these was the body of acrostics, made up of very disproportioned persons. It was disposed into three columns, the officers planting themselves in a line on the left hand of each column. The officers were all of them at least six feet high, and made three rows of very proper men; but the common soldiers, who filled up the spaces between the officers, were such dwarfs, cripples, and scarecrows, that one could hardly look upon them without laughing. There were behind the acrostics two or three files of chronograms, which differed only from the former as their officers were equipped, like the figure of Time, with an hour-glass in one hand, and a scythe in the other, and took their posts promiscuously among the private men whom they commanded.

In the body of the temple, and before the very face of the deity, methought I saw the phantom of Tryphiodorus, the lipogrammatist, engaged in a ball with four-and-twenty persons, who pursued him by turns through all the intricacies and labyrinths of a country dance, without being able to overtake him.

Observing several to be very busy at the western end of the temple, I inquired into what they were doing, and found there was in that quarter the great magazine of rebuses. These were several things of the most different natures tied up in bundles, and thrown upon one another in heaps like fagots. You might behold an anchor, a night-rail, and a hobby-horse bound up together. One of the workmen, seeing me very much surprised, told me there was an infinite deal of wit in several of those bundles, and that he would explain them to me if I pleased; I thanked him for his civility, but told him I was in very great haste at that time. As I was going out of the temple, I observed in one corner of it a cluster of men and women laughing very heartily, and diverting themselves at a game of crambo. I heard several double rhymes as I passed by them, which raised a great deal of mirth.

Not far from these was another set of merry people engaged at a diversion, in which the whole jest was to mistake one person for another. To give occasion for these ludicrous mistakes, they were divided into pairs, every pair being covered from head to foot with the same kind of dress, though perhaps there was not the least resemblance in their faces. By this means an old man was sometimes mistaken for a boy, a woman for a man, and a blackamoor for an European, which very often produced great peals of laughter. These I guessed to be a party of puns. But being very desirous to get out of this world of magic, which had almost turned my brain, I left the temple and crossed over the fields that lay about it with all the speed I could make. I was not gone far before I heard the sound of trumpets and alarms, which seemed to proclaim the march of an enemy : and, as I afterwards found, was in reality what I apprehended it. There appeared at a great distance a very shining light, and in the midst of it a person of a most beautiful aspect; her name was Truth. On her right hand there marched a male deity, who bore several quivers on his shoulders, and grasped several arrows in his hand; his name was Wit. The approach of these two enemies filled all the territories of False Wit with an unspeakable consternation, insomuch that the goddess of those regions appeared in person upon her frontiers, with the several inferior deities and the different bodies of forces which I had before seen in the temple, who were now drawn up in array, and prepared to give their foes a warm reception. As the march of the enemy was very slow, it gave time to the several inhabitants who bordered upon the regions of Falsehood to draw their forces into a body, with a design to stand upon their guard as neuters, and attend the issue of the combat.

I must here inform my reader that the frontiers of

the enchanted region, which I have before described, were inhabited by the species of Mixed Wit, who made a very odd appearance when they were mustered together in an army. There were men whose bodies were stuck full of darts, and women whose eyes were burning-glasses; men that had hearts of fire, and women that had breasts of snow. It would be endless to describe several monsters of the like nature that composed this great army, which immediately fell asunder, and divided itself into two parts, the one half throwing themselves behind the banners of Truth,. and the others behind those of Falsehood.

The goddess of Falsehood was of a gigantic stature, and advanced some paces before the front of the army ; but as the dazzling light which flowed from Truth. began to shine upon her, she faded insensibly ; insomuch that in a little space she looked rather like a huge phantom than a real substance. At length, as the goddess of Truth approached still nearer to her, she fell away entirely, and vanished amidst the brightness of her presence ; so that there did not remain the least trace or impression of her figure in the place where she had been seen.

As at the rising of the sun the constellations grow thin, and the stars go out one after another, till the whole hemisphere is extinguished; such was the vanishing of the goddess, and not only of the goddess herself, but of the whole army that attended her,

D—130

which sympathised with their leader, and shrunk into nothing, in proportion as the goddess disappeared. At the same time the whole temple sunk, the fish betook themselves to the streams, and the wild beasts to the woods, the fountains recovered their murmurs, the birds their voices, the trees their leaves, the flowers their scents, and the whole face of nature its true and genuine appearance. Though I still continued asleep, I fancied myself, as it were, awakened out of a dream, when I saw this region of prodigies restored to woods and rivers, fields and meadows.

Upon the removal of that wild scene of wonders, which had very much disturbed my imagination, I took a full survey of the persons of Wit and Truth; for indeed it was impossible to look upon the first without seeing the other at the same time. There was behind them a strong compact body of figures. The genius of Heroic Poetry appeared with a sword in her hand, and a laurel on her head. Tragedy was crowned with cypress, and covered with robes dipped in blood. Satire had smiles in her look, and a dagger under her garment. Rhetoric was known by her thunderbolt, and Comedy by her mask. After several other figures, Epigram marched up in the rear, who had been posted there at the beginning of the expedition, that he might not revolt to the enemy, whom he was suspected to favour in his heart. I was very much awed and delighted with the appearance of the god of Wit;

there was something so amiable, and yet so piercing, in his looks, as inspired me at once with love and terror. As I was gazing on him, to my unspeakable joy, he took a quiver of arrows from his shoulder, in order to make me a present of it; but as I was reaching out my hand to receive it of him, I knocked it against a chair, and by that means awaked.

FRIENDSHIP.

Nos duo turba sumus.

OVID, *Met.* i. 355.

We two are a multitude.

ONE would think that the larger the company is, in which we are engaged, the greater variety of thoughts and subjects would be started in discourse; but instead of this, we find that conversation is never so much straitened and confined as in numerous assemblies. When a multitude meet together upon any subject of discourse, their debates are taken up chiefly with forms and general positions; nay, if we come into a more contracted assembly of men and women, the talk generally runs upon the weather, fashions, news, and the like public topics. In proportion as conversation gets into clubs and knots of friends, it descends into particulars, and grows more free and communicative: but the most open, instructive, and unreserved discourse is that which passes between two persons who are familiar and intimate friends. On these occasions, a man gives a loose to every passion and every thought that is uppermost, discovers his most retired opinions of persons and things, tries the beauty and strength of his sentiments, and exposes his whole soul to the examination of his friend.

Tully was the first who observed that friendship improves happiness and abates misery, by the doubling of our joy and dividing of our grief; a thought in which he hath been followed, by all the essayists upon friendship that have written since his time. Sir Francis Bacon has finely described other advantages, or, as he calls them, fruits of friendship; and, indeed, there is no subject of morality which has been better handled and more exhausted than this. Among the several fine things which have been spoken of it, I shall beg leave to quote some out of a very ancient author, whose book would be regarded by our modern wits as one of the most shining tracts of morality that is extant, if it appeared under the name of a Confucius, or of any celebrated Grecian philosopher; I mean the little apocryphal treatise entitled The Wisdom of the Son of Sirach. How finely has he described the art of making friends by an obliging and affable behaviour; and laid down that precept, which

a late excellent author has delivered as his own, That
we should have many well-wishers, but few friends.
"Sweet language will multiply friends; and a fair-
speaking tongue will increase kind greetings. Be in
peace with many, nevertheless have but one counsellor
of a thousand." With what prudence does he caution
us in the choice of our friends! And with what
strokes of nature, I could almost say of humour, has
he described the behaviour of a treacherous and self-
interested friend! "If thou wouldest get a friend,
prove him first, and be not hasty to credit him: for
some man is a friend for his own occasion, and will
not abide in the day of thy trouble. And there is a
friend who, being turned to enmity and strife, will
discover thy reproach." Again, "Some friend is a
companion at the table, and will not continue in the
day of thy affliction: but in thy prosperity he will be
as thyself, and will be bold over thy servants. If thou
be brought low, he will be against thee, and hide
himself from thy face." What can be more strong and
pointed than the following verse?—"Separate thyself
from thine enemies, and take heed of thy friends." In
the next words he particularises one of those fruits of
friendship which is described at length by the two
famous authors above-mentioned, and falls into a
general eulogium of friendship, which is very just as
well as very sublime. "A faithful friend is a strong
defence; and he that hath found such an one hath

found a treasure. Nothing doth countervail a faithful
friend, and his excellency is unvaluable. A faithful
friend is the medicine of life; and they that fear the
Lord shall find him. Whoso feareth the Lord shall
direct his friendship aright; for as he is, so shall his
neighbour, that is his friend, be also." I do not remember to have met with any saying that has pleased
me more than that of a friend's being the medicine of
life, to express the efficacy of friendship in healing the
pains and anguish which naturally cleave to our existence in this world; and am wonderfully pleased with
the turn in the last sentence, that a virtuous man shall
as a blessing meet with a friend who is as virtuous as
himself. There is another saying in the same author,
which would have been very much admired in a
heathen writer: "Forsake not an old friend, for the
new is not comparable to him: a new friend is as new
wine; when it is old thou shalt drink it with pleasure."
With what strength of allusion and force of thought
has he described the breaches and violations of friendship!—" Whoso casteth a stone at the birds, frayeth
them away; and he that upbraideth his friend,
breaketh friendship. Though thou drawest a sword at
a friend, yet despair not, for there may be a returning
to favour. If thou hast opened thy mouth against thy
friend, fear not, for there may be a reconciliation:
except for upbraiding, or pride, or disclosing of secrets,
or a treacherous wound; for, for these things every

friend will depart." We may observe in this, and several other precepts in this author, those little familiar instances and illustrations which are so much admired in the moral writings of Horace and Epictetus. There are very beautiful instances of this nature in the following passages, which are likewise written upon the same subject: " Whoso discovereth secrets, loseth his credit, and shall never find a friend to his mind. Love thy friend, and be faithful unto him; but if thou bewrayeth his secrets, follow no more after him: for as a man hath destroyed his enemy, so hast thou lost the love of thy friend; as one that letteth a bird go out of his hand, so hast thou let thy friend go, and shall not get him again: follow after him no more, for he is too far off; he is as a roe escaped out of the snare. As for a wound it may be bound up, and after reviling there may be reconciliation; but he that bewrayeth secrets, is without hope."

Among the several qualifications of a good friend, this wise man has very justly singled out constancy and faithfulness as the principal: to these, others have added virtue, knowledge, discretion, equality in age and fortune, and, as Cicero calls it, *Morum comitas*, "a pleasantness of temper." If I were to give my opinion upon such an exhausted subject, I should join to these other qualifications a certain equability or evenness of behaviour. A man often contracts a friendship with one whom perhaps he does not find out till after a year's conversation; when on a sudden some latent ill-humour breaks out upon him, which he never discovered or suspected at his first entering into an intimacy with him. There are several persons who in some certain periods of their lives are inexpressibly agreeable, and in others as odious and detestable. Martial has given us a very pretty picture of one of this species, in the following epigram:

Difficilis, facilis, jucundus, acerbus es idem,
Nec tecum possum vivere, nec sine te.

Ep. xii. 47.

In all thy humours, whether grave or mellow,
Thou'rt such a touchy, testy, pleasant fellow;
Hast so much wit, and mirth, and spleen about thee,
There is no living with thee, nor without thee.

It is very unlucky for a man to be entangled in a friendship with one who, by these changes and vicissitudes of humour, is sometimes amiable and sometimes odious: and as most men are at some times in admirable frame and disposition of mind, it should be one of the greatest tasks of wisdom to keep ourselves well when we are so, and never to go out of that which is the agreeable part of our character.

CHEVY-CHASE.

Interdum vulgus rectum videt.

HOR., *Ep.* ii. 1, 63.

Sometimes the vulgar see and judge aright.

WHEN I travelled I took a particular delight in hearing the songs and fables that are come from father to son, and are most in vogue among the common people of the countries through which I passed; for it is impossible that anything should be universally tasted and approved by a multitude, though they are only the rabble of a nation, which hath not in it some peculiar aptness to please and gratify the mind of man. Human nature is the same in all reasonable creatures; and whatever falls in with it will meet with admirers amongst readers of all qualities and conditions. Molière, as we are told by Monsieur Boileau, used to read all his comedies to an old woman who was his housekeeper as she sat with him at her work by the chimney-corner, and could foretell the success of his play in the theatre from the reception it met at his fireside; for he tells us the audience always followed the old woman, and never failed to laugh in the same place.

I know nothing which more shows the essential and inherent perfection of simplicity of thought, above that which I call the Gothic manner in writing, than this, that the first pleases all kinds of palates, and the latter only such as have formed to themselves a wrong artificial taste upon little fanciful authors and writers of epigram. Homer, Virgil, or Milton, so far as the language of their poems is understood, will please a reader of plain common sense, who would neither relish nor comprehend an epigram of Martial, or a poem of Cowley; so, on the contrary, an ordinary song or ballad that is the delight of the common people cannot fail to please all such readers as are not unqualified for the entertainment by their affectation of ignorance; and the reason is plain, because the same paintings of nature which recommend it to the most ordinary reader will appear beautiful to the most refined.

The old song of "Chevy-Chase" is the favourite ballad of the common people of England, and Ben Jonson used to say he had rather have been the author of it than of all his works. Sir Philip Sidney, in his discourse of Poetry, speaks of it in the following words: "I never heard the old song of Percy and Douglas that I found not my heart more moved than with a trumpet; and yet it is sung by some blind crowder with no rougher voice than rude style, which being so evil apparelled in the dust and cobweb of that uncivil age, what would it work trimmed in the gorgeous eloquence of Pindar?" For my own part, I am so professed an admirer of this antiquated song, that I shall give my reader a critique upon it without any further apology for so doing.

The greatest modern critics have laid it down as a rule that an heroic poem should be founded upon some important precept of morality adapted to the constitution of the country in which the poet writes. Homer and Virgil have formed their plans in this view. As Greece was a collection of many governments, who suffered very much among themselves, and gave the Persian emperor, who was their common enemy, many advantages over them by their mutual jealousies and animosities, Homer, in order to establish among them an union which was so necessary for their safety, grounds his poem upon the discords of the several Grecian princes who were engaged in a confederacy against an Asiatic prince, and the several advantages which the enemy gained by such discords. At the time the poem we are now treating of was written, the dissensions of the barons, who were then so many petty princes, ran very high, whether they quarrelled among themselves or with their neighbours, and produced unspeakable calamities to the country. The poet, to deter men from such unnatural contentions, describes a bloody battle and dreadful scene of death, occasioned by the mutual feuds which reigned in the families of an English and Scotch nobleman. That he designed this for the instruction of his poem we may learn from his four last lines, in which, after the example of the

modern tragedians, he draws from it a precept for the
benefit of his readers :

> God save the king, and bless the land
> In plenty, joy, and peace ;
> And grant henceforth that foul debate
> 'Twixt noblemen may cease.

The next point observed by the greatest heroic poets
hath been to celebrate persons and actions which do
honour to their country : thus Virgil's hero was the
founder of Rome; Homer's a prince of Greece ; and for
this reason Valerius Flaccus and Statius, who were
both Romans, might be justly derided for having
chosen the expedition of the Golden Fleece and the
Wars of Thebes for the subjects of their epic writings.

The poet before us has not only found out a hero in
his own country, but raises the reputation of it by
several beautiful incidents. The English are the first
who take the field and the last who quit it. The
English bring only fifteen hundred to the battle, the
Scotch two thousand. The English keep the field
with fifty-three, the Scotch retire with fifty-five ; all
the rest on each side being slain in battle. But the
most remarkable circumstance of this kind is the
different manner in which the Scotch and English
kings receive the news of this fight, and of the great
men's deaths who commanded in it :

> This news was brought to Edinburgh,
> Where Scotland's king did reign,

That brave Earl Douglas suddenly
  Was with an arrow slain.

" O heavy news ! " King James did say,
  " Scotland can witness be,
I have not any captain more
  Of such account as he."

Like tidings to King Henry came,
  Within as short a space,
That Percy of Northumberland
  Was slain in Chevy-Chase.

" Now God be with him," said our king,
  " Sith 'twill no better be,
I trust I have within my realm
  Five hundred as good as he.

" Yet shall not Scot nor Scotland say
  But I will vengeance take,
And be revenged on them all
  For brave Lord Percy's sake."

This vow full well the king performed
  After on Humble-down,
In one day fifty knights were slain,
  With lords of great renown.

And of the rest of small account
  Did many thousands die, &c.

At the same time that our poet shows a landable par-
tiality to his countrymen, he represents the Scots after
a manner not unbecoming so bold and brave a people :

Earl Douglas on a milk-white steed,
  Most like a baron bold,
Rode foremost of the company,
  Whose armour shone like gold.

His sentiments and actions are every way suitable to a
hero. "One of us two," says he, "must die: I am an
earl as well as yourself, so that you can have no pre-
tence for refusing the combat; however." says he, "it
is pity, and indeed would be a sin, that so many innocent men should perish for our sakes: rather let you
and I end our quarrel in single fight:"

" Ere thus I will out-braved be,
    One of us two shall die ;
I know thee well, an earl thou art,
    Lord Percy, so am I.

"But trust me, Percy, pity it were
    And great offence to kill
Any of these our harmless men,
    For they have done no ill.

" Let thou and I the battle try,
    And set our men aside."
"Accurst be he," Lord Percy said,
    " By whom this is deny'd."

When these brave men had distinguished themselves
in the battle and in single combat with each other, in
the midst of a generous parley, full of heroic sentiments, the Scotch earl falls, and with his dying words
encourages his men to revenge his death, representing
to them, as the most bitter circumstance of it, that his
rival saw him fall :

With that there came an arrow keen
    Out of an English bow,
Which struck Earl Douglas to the heart
    A deep and deadly blow.

Who never spoke more words than these,
" Fight on, my merry men all,
For why, my life is at an end,
Lord Percy sees my fall."

Merry men, in the language of those times, is no more
than a cheerful word for companions and fellow-
soldiers. A passage in the eleventh book of Virgil's
" Æneid " is very much to be admired, where Camilla,
in her last agonies, instead of weeping over the wound
she had received, as one might have expected from a
warrior of her sex, considers only, like the hero of
whom we are now speaking, how the battle should be
continued after her death :

Tum sic exspirans, &c.   VIRG., *Æn.* xi. 820.

A gath'ring mist o'erclouds her cheerful eyes ;
And from her cheeks the rosy colour flies,
Then turns to her, whom of her female train
She trusted most, and thus she speaks with pain :
" Acca, 'tis past ! he swims before my sight,
Inexorable Death, and claims his right.
Bear my last words to Turnus ; fly with speed
And bid him timely to my charge succeed ;
Repel the Trojans, and the town relieve :
Farewell."   DRYDEN.

Turnus did not die in so heroic a manner, though
our poet seems to have had his eye upon Turnus's
speech in the last verse :

Lord Percy sees my fall.

—*Vicisti, et victum tendere palmas
Ausonii videre.*   VIRG., *Æn.* xii. 936.

> The Latin chiefs have seen me beg my life.
>
> DRYDEN.

Earl Percy's lamentation over his enemy is generous, beautiful, and passionate. I must only caution the reader not to let the simplicity of the style, which one may well pardon in so old a poet, prejudice him against the greatness of the thought:

> Then leaving life, Earl Percy took
> The dead man by the hand,
> And said, "Earl Douglas, for thy life
> Would I had lost my land.
>
> "O Christ! my very heart doth bleed
> With sorrow for thy sake;
> For sure a more renowned knight
> Mischance did never take."

That beautiful line, "Taking the dead man by the hand," will put the reader in mind of Æneas's behaviour towards Lausus, whom he himself had slain as he came to the rescue of his aged father:

> At vero ut vultum vidit morientis et ora,
> Ora modis Anchisiades pallentia miris;
> Ingemuit, miserans graviter, dextramque tetendit.
>
> VIRG., Æn. x. 821.

> The pious prince beheld young Lausus dead;
> He grieved, he wept, then grasped his hand and said,
> "Poor hapless youth! what praises can be paid
> To worth so great?"
> DRYDEN.

I shall take another opportunity to consider the other parts of this old song.

—Pendent opera interrupta.

VIRG., *Æn.* iv. 88.

The works unfinished and neglected lie.

In my last Monday's paper I gave some general instances of those beautiful strokes which please the reader in the old song of " Chevy-Chase ;" I shall here, according to my promise, be more particular, and show that the sentiments in that ballad are extremely natural and poetical, and full of the majestic simplicity which we admire in the greatest of the ancient poets : for which reason I shall quote several passages of it, in which the thought is altogether the same with what we meet in several passages of the " Æneid ; " not that I would infer from thence that the poet, whoever he was, proposed to himself any imitation of those passages, but that he was directed to them in general by the same kind of poetical genius, and by the same copyings after nature.

Had this old song been filled with epigrammatical turns and points of wit, it might perhaps have pleased the wrong taste of some readers ; but it would never have become the delight of the common people, nor have warmed the heart of Sir Philip Sidney like the sound of a trumpet; it is only nature that can have this effect, and please those tastes which are the most unprejudiced, or the most refined. I must, however, beg leave to dissent from so great an authority as that of Sir Philip Sidney, in the judgment which he has passed as to the rude style and evil apparel of this antiquated song; for there are several parts in it where not only the thought but the language is majestic, and the numbers sonorous; at least the apparel is much more gorgeous than many of the poets made use of in Queen Elizabeth's time, as the reader will see in several of the following quotations.

What can be greater than either the thought or the expression in that stanza,

> To drive the deer with hound and horn
> Earl Percy took his way ;
> The child may rue that is unborn
> The hunting of that day !

This way of considering the misfortunes which this battle would bring upon posterity, not only on those who were born immediately after the battle, and lost their fathers in it, but on those also who perished in future battles which took their rise from this quarrel of the two earls, is wonderfully beautiful and conformable to the way of thinking among the ancient poets.

> *Audiet pugnas vitio parentum*
> *Rara juventus.*
> HOR., *Od.* i. 2, 23.

> Posterity, thinn'd by their fathers' crimes,
> ' Shall read, with grief, the story of their times.

What can be more sounding and poetical, or resemble more the majestic simplicity of the ancients, than the following stanzas?—

The stout Earl of Northumberland
 A vow to God did make,
His pleasure in the Scottish woods
 Three summer's days to take.

With fifteen hundred bowmen bold,
 All chosen men of might,
Who knew full well, in time of need,
 To aim their shafts aright.

The hounds ran swiftly through the woods
 The nimble deer to take,
And with their cries the hills and dales
 An echo shrill did make.

> —*Vocat ingenti clamore Cithæron,*
> *Taygetique canes, domitrixque Epidaurus equorum :*
> *Et vox assensu nemorum ingeminata remugit.*
> VIRG., Georg. iii. 43.

Cithæron loudly calls me to my way :
Thy hounds, Taygetus, open, and pursue their prey :
High Epidaurus urges on my speed,
Famed for his hills, and for his horses' breed :
From hills and dales the cheerful cries rebound :
For Echo hunts along, and propagates the sound.
DRYDEN.

Lo, yonder doth Earl Douglas come,
 His men in armour bright ;
Full twenty hundred Scottish spears,
 All marching in our sight.

All men of pleasant Tividale,
 Fast by the river Tweed, &c.

The country of the Scotch warrior, described in these two last verses, has a fine romantic situation, and affords a couple of smooth words for verse. If the reader compares the foregoing six lines of the song with the following Latin verses, he will see how much they are written in the spirit of Virgil :

Adversi campo apparent : hastasque reductis
Protendunt longè dextris, et spicula vibrant :—
Quique altum Præneste viri, quique arva Gabinæ
Junonis, gelidumque Anienem, et roscida rivis
Hernica saxa colunt :—qui rosea rura Velini ;
Qui Tetricæ horrentes rupes, montemque Severum,
Casperiamque colunt, Forulosque et flumen Himellæ :
Qui Tyberim Fabarimque bibunt.

Æn. xi. 605, vii. 682, 712.

Advancing in a line they couch their spears——
——Præneste sends a chosen band,
With those who plough Saturnia's Gabine land :
Besides the succours which cold Anien yields :
The rocks of Hernicus—besides a band
That followed from Velinum's dewy land—
And mountaineers that from Severus came :
And from the craggy cliffs of Tetrica ;
And those where yellow Tiber takes his way,
And where Himella's wanton waters play :
Casperia sends her arms, with those that lie
By Fabaris, and fruitful Foruli.

DRYDEN.

But to proceed :

Earl Douglas on a milk-white steed,
 Most like a baron bold,
Rode foremost of the company,
 Whose armour shone like gold.

Turnus, ut antevolans tardum præcesserat agmen, &c.
Vidisti, quo Turnus equo, quibus ibat in armis
Aureus—

Æn. ix. 47, 269.

Our English archers bent their bows,
    Their hearts were good and true ;
At the first flight of arrows sent,
    Full threescore Scots they slew.

They closed full fast on ev'ry side,
    No slackness there was found ;
And many a gallant gentleman
    Lay gasping on the ground.

With that there came an arrow keen
    Out of an English bow,
Which struck Earl Douglas to the heart,
    A deep and deadly blow.

Æneas was wounded after the same manner by an unknown hand in the midst of a parley.

Has inter voces, media inter talia verba,
Ecce viro stridens alis allapsa sagitta est,
Incertum quâ pulsa manu —
                     Æn. xii. 318.

Thus, while he spake, unmindful of defence,
A winged arrow struck the pious prince ;
But whether from a human hand it came,
Or hostile god, is left unknown by fame.
                             DRYDEN.

But of all the descriptive parts of this song, there are none more beautiful than the four following stanzas, which have a great force and spirit in them, and are filled with very natural circumstances. The thought in the third stanza was never touched by any other poet, and is such a one as would have shone in Homer or in Virgil :

So thus did both these nobles die,
　Whose courage none could stain ;
An English archer then perceived
　The noble Earl was slain.

He had a bow bent in his hand,
　Made of a trusty tree,
An arrow of a cloth-yard long
　Unto the head drew he.

Against Sir Hugh Montgomery
　So right his shaft he set,
The gray-goose wing that was thereon
　In his heart-blood was wet.

This fight did last from break of day
　Till setting of the sun ;
For when they rung the ev'ning bell
　The battle scarce was done.

One may observe, likewise, that in the catalogue of
the slain, the author has followed the example of the
greatest ancient poets, not only in giving a long list
of the dead, but by diversifying it with little characters of particular persons.

And with Earl Douglas there was slain
　Sir Hugh Montgomery,
Sir Charles Carrel, that from the field
　One foot would never fly.

Sir Charles Murrel of Ratcliff too,
　His sister's son was he ;
Sir David Lamb so well esteem'd,
　Yet saved could not be.

The familiar sound in these names destroys the majesty

of the description; for this reason I do not mention
this part of the poem but to show the natural cast of
thought which appears in it, as the two last verses look
almost like a translation of Virgil.

—*Cadit et Ripheus justissimus unus*
Qui fuit in Teucris et servantissimus æqui.
Diis aliter visum.

                                                    Æn. ii. 426.

Then Ripheus fell in the unequal fight,
Just of his word, observant of the right :
Heav'n thought not so.

                                                    DRYDEN.

In the catalogue of the English who fell, Withering-
ton's behaviour is in the same manner particularised
very artfully, as the reader is prepared for it by that
account which is given of him in the beginning of the
battle; though I am satisfied your little buffoon readers,
who have seen that passage ridiculed in "Hudibras,"
will not be able to take the beauty of it : for which
reason I dare not so much as quote it.

Then stept a gallant 'squire forth,
    Witherington was his name,
Who said, "I would not have it told
    To Henry our king for shame,

"That e'er my captain fought on foot,
    And I stood looking on."

We meet with the same heroic sentiment in Virgil:

Non pudet, O Rutuli, cunctis pro talibus unam
Objectare animam ? numerone an viribus æqui
Non sumus ?

Æn. xii. 229

For shame, Rutilians, can you bear the sight
Of one exposed for all, in single fight ?
Can we before the face of heav'n confess
Our courage colder, or our numbers less ?

DRYDEN.

What can be more natural, or more moving, than the
circumstances in which he describes the behaviour of
those women who had lost their husbands on this fatal
day ?

Next day did many widows come
　　Their husbands to bewail ;
They wash'd their wounds in brinish tears,
　　But all would not prevail.

Their bodies bathed in purple blood,
　　They bore with them away ;
They kiss'd them dead a thousand times,
　　When they were clad in clay.

Thus we see how the thoughts of this poem, which
naturally arise from the subject, are always simple,
and sometimes exquisitely noble ; that the language is
often very sounding, and that the whole is written with
a true poetical spirit.

If this song had been written in the Gothic manner,
which is the delight of all our little wits, whether
writers or readers, it would not have hit the taste of
so many ages, and have pleased the readers of all ranks

and conditions. I shall only beg pardon for such a profusion of Latin quotations; which I should not have made use of, but that I feared my own judgment would have looked too singular on such a subject, had not I supported it by the practice and authority of Virgil.

A DREAM OF THE PAINTERS.

—Animum pictura pascit inani.

VIRG., Æn. i. 464.

And with the shadowy picture feeds his mind.

WHEN the weather hinders me from taking my diversions without-doors, I frequently make a little party, with two or three select friends, to visit anything curious that may be seen under cover. My principal entertainments of this nature are pictures, insomuch that when I have found the weather set in to be very bad, I have taken a whole day's journey to see a gallery that is furnished by the hands of great masters. By this means, when the heavens are filled with clouds, when the earth swims in rain, and all nature wears a lowering countenance, I withdraw myself from these uncomfortable scenes, into the visionary worlds of art; where I meet with shining landscapes, gilded triumphs, beautiful faces, and all those other objects that fill the mind with gay ideas, and disperse that gloominess which is apt to hang upon it in those dark disconsolate seasons.

I was some weeks ago in a course of these diversions, which had taken such an entire possession of my imagination that they formed in it a short morning's dream, which I shall communicate to my reader, rather as the first sketch and outlines of a vision, than as a finished piece.

I dreamt that I was admitted into a long, spacious gallery, which had one side covered with pieces of all the famous painters who are now living, and the other with the works of the greatest masters that are dead.

On the side of the living, I saw several persons busy in drawing, colouring, and designing. On the side of the dead painters, I could not discover more than one person at work, who was exceeding slow in his motions, and wonderfully nice in his touches.

I was resolved to examine the several artists that stood before me, and accordingly applied myself to the side of the living. The first I observed at work in this part of the gallery was Vanity, with his hair tied behind him in a riband, and dressed like a Frenchman. All the faces he drew were very remarkable for their smiles, and a certain smirking air which he bestowed indifferently on every age and degree of either sex. The *toujours gai* appeared

even in his judges, bishops, and Privy Councillors.
In a word, all his men were *petits maitres*, and all
his women *coquettes*. The drapery of his figures was
extremely well suited to his faces, and was made up
of all the glaring colours that could be mixed together; every part of the dress was in a flutter, and
endeavoured to distinguish itself above the rest.

On the left hand of Vanity stood a laborious workman, who I found was his humble admirer, and
copied after him. He was dressed like a German, and
had a very hard name that sounded something like
Stupidity.

The third artist that I looked over was Fantasque,
dressed like a Venetian scaramouch. He had an excellent hand at chimera, and dealt very much in distortions and grimaces. He would sometimes affright
himself with the phantoms that flowed from his
pencil. In short, the most elaborate of his pieces
was at best but a terrifying dream: and one could
say nothing more of his finest figures than that they
were agreeable monsters.

The fourth person I examined was very remarkable for his hasty hand, which left his pictures so
unfinished that the beauty in the picture, which was
designed to continue as a monument of it to posterity,
faded sooner than in the person after whom it was
drawn. He made so much haste to despatch his
business that he neither gave himself time to clean his

pencils nor mix his colours. The name of this expeditious workman was Avarice.

Not far from this artist I saw another of a quite different nature, who was dressed in the habit of a Dutchman, and known by the name of Industry. His figures were wonderfully laboured. If he drew the portraiture of a man, he did not omit a single hair in his face; if the figure of a ship, there was not a rope among the tackle that escaped him. He had likewise hung a great part of the wall with night-pieces, that seemed to show themselves by the candles which were lighted up in several parts of them; and were so inflamed by the sunshine which accidentally fell upon them, that at first sight I could scarce forbear crying out " Fire !"

The five foregoing artists were the most considerable on this side the gallery; there were indeed several others whom I had not time to look into. One of them, however, I could not forbear observing, who was very busy in retouching the finest pieces, though he produced no originals of his own. His pencil aggravated every feature that was before overcharged, loaded every defect, and poisoned every colour it touched. Though this workman did so much mischief on the side of the living, he never turned his eye towards that of the dead. His name was Envy.

Having taken a cursory view of one side of the

gallery, I turned myself to that which was filled by the works of those great masters that were dead; when immediately I fancied myself standing before a multitude of spectators, and thousands of eyes looking upon me at once: for all before me appeared so like men and women, that I almost forgot they were pictures. Raphael's pictures stood in one row, Titian's in another, Guido Rheni's in a third. One part of the wall was peopled by Hannabal Carrache, another by Correggio, and another by Rubens. To be short, there was not a great master among the dead who had not contributed to the embellishment of this side of the gallery. The persons that owed their being to these several masters appeared all of them to be real and alive, and differed among one another only in the variety of their shapes, complexions, and clothes; so that they looked like different nations of the same species.

Observing an old man, who was the same person I before mentioned, as the only artist that was at work on this side of the gallery, creeping up and down from one picture to another, and retouching all the fine pieces that stood before me, I could not but be very attentive to all his motions. I found his pencil was so very light that it worked imperceptibly, and after a thousand touches scarce produced any visible effect in the picture on which he was employed. However, as he busied himself incessantly, and repeated touch after touch without rest or intermission, he wore off insensibly every little disagreeable gloss that hung upon a figure. He also added such a beautiful brown to the shades, and mellowness to the colours, that he made every picture appear more perfect than when it came fresh from the master's pencil. I could not forbear looking upon the face of this ancient workman, and immediately, by the long lock of hair upon his forehead, discovered him to be Time.

Whether it were because the thread of my dream was at an end I cannot tell, but, upon my taking a survey of this imaginary old man, my sleep left me.

SPARE TIME.

—*Spatio brevi*
Spem longam reseces : dum loquimur, fugerit invida
Ætas : carpe diem, quàm minimum credula postero.

HOR., *Od.* i. 11, 6.

Thy lengthen'd hope with prudence bound,
   Proportion'd to the flying hour :
While thus we talk in careless ease,
   Our envious minutes wing their flight ;
Then swift the fleeting pleasure seize,
   Nor trust to-morrow's doubtful light.

FRANCIS.

WE all of us complain of the shortness of time, saith Seneca, and yet have much more than we know what

to do with. Our lives, says he, are spent either in
doing nothing at all, or in doing nothing to the purpose, or in doing nothing that we ought to do. We
are always complaining our days are few, and acting as
though there would be no end of them. That noble
philosopher described our inconsistency with ourselves
in this particular, by all those various turns of expression and thoughts which are peculiar to his writings.

I often consider mankind as wholly inconsistent with
itself in a point that bears some affinity to the former.
Though we seem grieved at the shortness of life in
general, we are wishing every period of it at an end.
The minor longs to be of age, then to be a man of
business, then to make up an estate, then to arrive at
honours, then to retire. Thus, although the whole of
life is allowed by every one to be short, the several
divisions of it appear long and tedious. We are for
lengthening our span in general, but would fain contract the parts of which it is composed. The usurer
would be very well satisfied to have all the time
annihilated that lies between the present moment and
next quarter-day. The politician would be contented
to lose three years in his life, could he place things in
the posture which he fancies they will stand in after
such a revolution of time. The lover would be glad to
strike out of his existence all the moments that are to
pass away before the happy meeting. Thus, as fast as
our time runs, we should be very glad, in most part of

our lives, that it ran much faster than it does. Several hours of the day hang upon our hands, nay, we wish away whole years; and travel through time as through a country filled with many wild and empty wastes, which we would fain hurry over, that we may arrive at those several little settlements or imaginary points of rest which are dispersed up and down in it.

If we divide the life of most men into twenty parts, we shall find that at least nineteen of them are mere gaps and chasms, which are neither filled with pleasure nor business. I do not, however, include in this calculation the life of those men who are in a perpetual hurry of affairs, but of those only who are not always engaged in scenes of action; and I hope I shall not do an unacceptable piece of service to these persons, if I point out to them certain methods for the filling up their empty spaces of life. The methods I shall propose to them are as follow.

The first is the exercise of virtue, in the most general acceptation of the word. That particular scheme which comprehends the social virtues may give employment to the most industrious temper, and find a man in business more than the most active station of life. To advise the ignorant, relieve the needy, comfort the afflicted, are duties that fall in our way almost every day of our lives. A man has frequent opportunities of mitigating the fierceness of a party; of doing justice to the character of a deserving man; of softening the

envious, quieting the angry, and rectifying the pre-
judiced; which are all of them employments suited to a
reasonable nature, and bring great satisfaction to the
person who can busy himself in them with discretion.

There is another kind of virtue that may find employment for those retired hours in which we are
altogether left to ourselves, and destitute of company
and conversation; I mean that intercourse and communication which every reasonable creature ought to
maintain with the great Author of his being. The
man who lives under an habitual sense of the Divine
presence, keeps up a perpetual cheerfulness of temper,
and enjoys every moment the satisfaction of· thinking
himself in company with his dearest and best of friends.
The time never lies heavy upon him: it is impossible
for him to be alone. His thoughts and passions are
the most busied at such hours when those of other men
are the most inactive. He no sooner steps out of the
world but his heart burns with devotion, swells with
hope, and triumphs in the consciousness of that Presence which everywhere surrounds him; or, on the
contrary, pours out its fears, its sorrows, its apprehensions, to the great Supporter of its existence.

I have here only considered the necessity of a man's
being virtuous, that he may have something to do; but
if we consider further that the exercise of virtue is not
only an amusement for the time it lasts, but that its
influence extends to those parts of our existence which

lie beyond the grave, and that our whole eternity is to take its colour from those hours which we here employ in virtue or in vice, the argument redoubles upon us for putting in practice this method of passing away our time.

When a man has but a little stock to improve, and has opportunities of turning it all to good account, what shall we think of him if he suffers nineteen parts of it to lie dead, and perhaps employs even the twentieth to his ruin or disadvantage? But, because the mind cannot be always in its fervours, nor strained up to a pitch of virtue, it is necessary to find out proper employments for it in its relaxations.

The next method, therefore, that I would propose to fill up our time, should be useful and innocent diversions. I must confess I think it is below reasonable creatures to be altogether conversant in such diversions as are merely innocent, and have nothing else to recommend them but that there is no hurt in them. Whether any kind of gaming has even thus much to say for itself, I shall not determine; but I think it is very wonderful to see persons of the best sense passing away a dozen hours together in shuffling and dividing a pack of cards, with no other conversation but what is made up of a few game phrases, and no other ideas but those of black or red spots ranged together in different figures. Would not a man laugh to hear any one of this species complaining that life is short?

The stage might be made a perpetual source of the

most noble and useful entertainments, were it under proper regulations.

But the mind never unbends itself so agreeably as in the conversation of a well-chosen friend. There is indeed no blessing of life that is any way comparable to the enjoyment of a discreet and virtuous friend. It eases and unloads the mind, clears and improves the understanding, engenders thoughts and knowledge, animates virtue and good resolutions, soothes and allays the passions, and finds employment for most of the vacant hours of life.

Next to such an intimacy with a particular person, one would endeavour after a more general conversation with such as are able to entertain and improve those with whom they converse, which are qualifications that seldom go asunder.

There are many other useful amusements of life which one would endeavour to multiply, that one might on all occasions have recourse to something rather than suffer the mind to lie idle, or run adrift with any passion that chances to rise in it.

A man that has a taste of music, painting, or architecture, is like one that has another sense, when compared with such as have no relish of those arts. The florist, the planter, the gardener, the husbandman, when they are only as accomplishments to the man of fortune, are great reliefs to a country life, and many ways useful to those who are possessed of them.

But of all the diversions of life, there is none so proper to fill up its empty spaces as the reading of useful and entertaining authors. But this I shall only touch upon, because it in some measure interferes with the third method, which I shall propose in another paper, for the employment of our dead, inactive hours, and which I shall only mention in general to be the pursuit of knowledge.

————

— *Hoc est*
Vivere bis, vitâ posse priore frui.
MART., *Ep.* x. 23.

The present joys of life we doubly taste,
By looking back with pleasure to the past.

THE last method which I proposed in my Saturday's paper, for filling up those empty spaces of life which are so tedious and burthensome to idle people, is the employing ourselves in the pursuit of knowledge. I remember Mr. Boyle, speaking of a certain mineral, tells us that a man may consume his whole life in the study of it without arriving at the knowledge of all its qualities. The truth of it is, there is not a single science, or any branch of it, that might not furnish a man with business for life, though it were much longer than it is.

I shall not here engage on those beaten subjects of the usefulness of knowledge, nor of the pleasure and

perfection it gives the mind, nor on the methods of
attaining it, nor recommend any particular branch of
it; all which have been the topics of many other
writers; but shall indulge myself in a speculation that
is more uncommon, and may therefore, perhaps, be more
entertaining.

I have before shown how the unemployed parts of
life appear long and tedious, and shall here endeavour
to show how those parts of life which are exercised in
study, reading, and the pursuits of knowledge, are
long, but not tedious, and by that means discover a
method of lengthening our lives, and at the same time
of turning all the parts of them to our advantage.

Mr. Locke observes, "That we get the idea of
time or duration, by reflecting on that train of ideas
which succeed one another in our minds: that, for
this reason, when we sleep soundly without dreaming,
we have no perception of time, or the length of it
whilst we sleep; and that the moment wherein we
leave off to think, till the moment we begin to think
again, seems to have no distance." To which the
author adds, "and so I doubt not but it would be to a
waking man, if it were possible for him to keep only
one idea in his mind, without variation and the succession of others; and we see that one who fixes his
thoughts very intently on one thing, so as to take but
little notice of the succession of ideas that pass in his
mind whilst he is taken up with that earnest contem-

plation, lets slip out of his account a good part of that duration, and thinks that time shorter than it is."

We might carry this thought further, and consider a man as on one side, shortening his time by thinking on nothing, or but a few things; so, on the other, as lengthening it, by employing his thoughts on many subjects, or by entertaining a quick and constant succession of ideas. Accordingly, Monsieur Malebranche, in his "Inquiry after Truth," which was published several years before Mr. Locke's Essay on "Human Understanding," tells us, "that it is possible some creatures may think half an hour as long as we do a thousand years; or look upon that space of duration which we call a minute, as an hour, a week, a month, or a whole age."

This notion of Monsieur Malebranche is capable of some little exp'anation from what I have quoted out of Mr. Locke; for if our notion of time is produced by our reflecting on the succession of ideas in our mind, and this succession may be infinitely accelerated or retarded, it will follow that different beings may have different notions of the same parts of duration, according as their ideas, which we suppose are equally distinct in each of them, follow one another in a greater or less degree of rapidity.

There is a famous passage in the Alcoran, which looks as if Mahomet had been possessed of the notion we are now speaking of. It is there said that the

Angel Gabriel took Mahomet out of his bed one morning to give him a sight of all things in the seven heavens, in paradise, and in hell, which the prophet took a distinct view of; and, after having held ninety thousand conferences with God, was brought back again to his bed. All this, says the Alcoran, was transacted in so small a space of time, that Mahomet at his return found his bed still warm, and took up an earthen pitcher, which was thrown down at the very instant that the Angel Gabriel carried him away, before the water was all spilt.

There is a very pretty story in the Turkish Tales, which relates to this passage of that famous impostor, and bears some affinity to the subject we are now upon. A sultan of Egypt, who was an infidel, used to laugh at this circumstance in Mahomet's life, as what was altogether impossible and absurd: but conversing one day with a great doctor in the law, who had the gift of working miracles, the doctor told him he would quickly convince him of the truth of this passage in the history of Mahomet, if he would consent to do what he should desire of him. Upon this the sultan was directed to place himself by a huge tub of water, which he did accordingly; and as he stood by the tub amidst a circle of his great men, the holy man bade him plunge his head into the water and draw it up again. The king accordingly thrust his head into the water, and at the same time found himself at the foot of a mountain on the sea-shore. The king immediately began to rage against his doctor for this piece of treachery and witchcraft; but at length, knowing it was in vain to be angry, he set himself to think on proper methods for getting a livelihood in this strange country. Accordingly he applied himself to some people whom he saw at work in a neighbouring wood: these people conducted him to a town that stood at a little distance from the wood, where, after some adventures, he married a woman of great beauty and fortune. He lived with this woman so long that he had by her seven sons and seven daughters. He was afterwards reduced to great want, and forced to think of plying in the streets as a porter for his livelihood. One day as he was walking alone by the sea-side, being seized with many melancholy reflections upon his former and his present state of life, which had raised a fit of devotion in him, he threw off his clothes with a design to wash himself, according to the custom of the Mahometans, before he said his prayers.

After his first plunge into the sea, he no sooner raised his head above the water but he found himself standing by the side of the tub, with the great men of his court about him, and the holy man at his side. He immediately upbraided his teacher for having sent him on such a course of adventures, and betrayed him into so long a state of misery and servitude; but was wonderfully surprised when he heard that the state he talked of was only a dream and delusion; that he had not stirred from the place where he then stood; and that he had only dipped his head into the water, and immediately taken it out again.

The Mahometan doctor took this occasion of instructing the sultan that nothing was impossible with God: and that He, with whom a thousand years are but as one day, can, if He pleases, make a single day—nay, a single moment—appear to any of His creatures as a thousand years.

I shall leave my reader to compare these Eastern fables with the notions of those two great philosophers whom I have quoted in this paper; and shall only, by way of application, desire him to consider how we may extend life beyond its natural dimensions, by applying ourselves diligently to the pursuit of knowledge.

The hours of a wise man are lengthened by his ideas, as those of a fool are by his passions. The time of the one is long, because he does not know what to do with it; so is that of the other, because he distinguishes every moment of it with useful or amusing thoughts: or, in other words, because the one is always wishing it away, and the other always enjoying it.

How different is the view of past life, in the man who is grown old in knowledge and wisdom, from that of him who is grown old in ignorance and folly! The latter is like the owner of a barren conutry, that fills his eye with the prospect of naked hills and plains, which produce nothing either profitable or ornamental; the other beholds a beautiful and spacious landscape divided into delightful gardens, green meadows, fruitful fields, and can scarce cast his eye on a single spot of his possessions that is not covered with some beautiful plant or flower.

CENSURE.

Romulus, et Liber pater, et cum Castore Pollux,
Post ingentia facta, deorum in templa recepti;
Dum terras hominumque colunt genus, aspera bella
Componunt, agros assignant, oppida condunt;
Ploravere suis non respondere favorem
Speratum meritis.
HOR., Epist. ii. 1, 5.

IMITATED.

Edward and Henry, now the boast of fame,
And virtuous Alfred, a more sacred name,
After a life of generous toils endured,
The Gaul subdued, or property secured,
Ambition humbled, mighty cities storm'd,
Or laws establish'd, and the world reform'd;
Closed their long glories with a sigh to find
Th' unwilling gratitude of base mankind.
POPE.

" CENSURE," says a late ingenious author, "is the tax a man pays to the public for being eminent." It is a folly for an eminent man to think of escaping it, and a weakness to be affected with it. All the illustrious persons of antiquity, and indeed of every age in the world, have passed through this fiery persecution. There is no defence against reproach but obscurity; it is a kind of concomitant to greatness, as satires and invectives were an essential part of a Roman triumph.

If men of eminence are exposed to censure on one hand, they are as much liable to flattery on the other. If they receive reproaches which are not due to them, they likewise receive praises which they do not deserve. In a word, the man in a high post is never regarded with an indifferent eye, but always considered as a friend or an enemy. For this reason persons in great stations have seldom their true characters drawn till several years after their deaths. Their personal friendships and enmities must cease, and the parties they were engaged in be at an end, before their faults or their virtues can have justice done them. When writers have the least opportunity of knowing the truth, they are in the best disposition to tell it.

It is therefore the privilege of posterity to adjust the characters of illustrious persons, and to set matters right between those antagonists who by their rivalry for greatness divided a whole age into factions. We can now allow Cæsar to be a great man, without derogating from Pompey; and celebrate the virtues of Cato, without detracting from those of Cæsar. Every one that has been long dead has a due proportion of praise allotted him, in which, whilst he lived, his friends were too profuse, and his enemies too sparing.

According to Sir Isaac Newton's calculations, the last comet that made its appearance, in 1680, imbibed so much heat by its approaches to the sun, that it would have been two thousand times hotter than red-hot iron, had it been a globe of that metal; and that supposing it as big as the earth, and at the same distance from the sun, it would be fifty thousand years in cooling, before it recovered its natural temper. In the like manner, if an Englishman considers the great ferment into which our political world is thrown at present, and how intensely it is heated in all its parts, he cannot suppose that it will cool again in less than three hundred years. In such a tract of time it is possible that the heats of the present age may be extinguished, and our several classes of great men represented under their proper characters. Some eminent historian may then probably arise that will not write *recentibus odiis*, as Tacitus expresses it, with the passions and prejudices of a contemporary author, but make an impartial distribution of fame among the great men of the present age.

I cannot forbear entertaining myself very often with the idea of such an imaginary historian describing the reign of Anne the First, and introducing it with a preface to his reader, that he is now entering upon the most shining part of the English story. The great rivals in fame will be then distinguished according to their respective merits, and shine in their proper points of light. Such an one, says the historian, though variously represented by the writers of his own age, appears to have been a man of more than ordinary abilities, great application, and uncommon integrity : nor was such an one, though of an opposite party and interest, inferior to him in any of these respects. The several antagonists who now endeavour to depreciate one another, and are celebrated or traduced by different parties, will then have the same body of admirers, and appear illustrious in the opinion of the whole British nation. The deserving man, who can now recommend himself to the esteem of but half his countrymen, will then receive the approbations and applauses of a whole age.

Among the several persons that flourish in this glorious reign, there is no question but such a future historian, as the person of whom I am speaking, will make mention of the men of genius and learning who have now any figure in the British nation. For my own part, I often flatter myself with the honourable mention which will then be made of me; and have drawn up a paragraph in my own imagination, that I fancy will not be altogether unlike what will be found in some page or other of this imaginary historian.

It was under this reign, says he, that the *Spectator* published those little diurnal essays which are still extant. We know very little of the name or person of this author, except only that he was a man of a very short face, extremely addicted to silence, and so great a lover of knowledge, that he made a voyage to Grand Cairo for no other reason but to take the measure of a pyramid. His chief friend was one Sir Roger De Coverley, a whimsical country knight, and a Templar, whose name he has not transmitted to us. He lived as a lodger at the house of a widow-woman, and was a great humorist in all parts of his life. This is all we can affirm with any certainty of his person and character. As for his speculations, notwithstanding the several obsolete words and obscure phrases of the age in which he lived, we still understand enough of them to see the diversions and characters of the English nation in his time : not but that we are to make allowance for the mirth and humour of the author, who has doubtless strained many representations of things beyond the truth. For if we interpret his words in their literal meaning, we must suppose that women 'of the first quality used to pass away whole mornings at a puppet-show ; that they attested their principles by their patches ; that an audience would sit out an evening to hear a dramatical performance written in a language which they did not understand ; that chairs and flower-pots were introduced as actors upon the British stage ; that a promiscuous assembly of men and women were allowed to meet at

midnight in masks within the verge of the Court; with
many improbabilities of the like nature. We must
therefore, in these and the like cases, suppose that these
remote hints and allusions aimed at some certain follies
which were then in vogue, and which at present we have
not any notion of. We may guess by several passages in the speculations, that there were writers who
endeavoured to detract from the works of this author;
but as nothing of this nature is come down to us, we
cannot guess at any objections that could be made to
his paper. If we consider his style with that in-
dulgence which we must show to old English writers,
or if we look into the variety of his subjects, with
those several critical dissertations, moral reflections,

*   *   *   *   *   *   *

The following part of the paragraph is so much to
my advantage, and beyond anything I can pretend to,
that I hope my reader will excuse me for not insert-
ing it.

THE ENGLISH LANGUAGE.

Est brevitate opus, ut currat sententia.

HOR., *Sat.* i. 10, 9.

Let brevity despatch the rapid thought.

I HAVE somewhere read of an eminent person who used in his private offices of devotion to give thanks to Heaven that he was born a Frenchman: for my own part I look upon it as a peculiar blessing that I was born an Englishman. Among many other reasons, I think myself very happy in my country, as the language of it is wonderfully adapted to a man who is sparing of his words, and an enemy to loquacity.

As I have frequently reflected on my good fortune in this particular, I shall communicate to the public my speculations upon the English tongue, not doubting but they will be acceptable to all my curious readers.

The English delight in silence more than any other European nation, if the remarks which are made on us by foreigners are true. Our discourse is not kept up in conversation, but falls into more pauses and intervals than in our neighbouring countries; as it is observed that the matter of our writings is thrown much closer together, and lies in a narrower compass, than is usual in the works of foreign authors; for, to favour our natural taciturnity, when we are obliged to utter our thoughts we do it in the shortest way we are able, and give as quick a birth to our conceptions as possible.

This humour shows itself in several remarks that we may make upon the English language. As, first of all, by its abounding in monosyllables, which gives us an opportunity of delivering our thoughts in few sounds. This indeed takes off from the elegance of our tongue, but at the same time expresses our ideas in the readiest manner, and consequently answers the first design of speech better than the multitude of syllables which make the words of other languages more tuneable and sonorous. The sounds of our English words are commonly like those of string music, short and transient, which rise and perish upon a single touch; those of other languages are like the notes of wind instruments, sweet and swelling, and lengthened out into variety of modulation.

In the next place we may observe that, where the words are not monosyllables, we often make them so, as much as lies in our power, by our rapidity of pronunciation; as it generally happens in most of our long words which are derived from the Latin, where we contract the length of the syllables, that gives them a grave and solemn air in their own language, to make them more proper for despatch, and more conformable to the genius of our tongue. This we may find in a multitude of words, as " liberty," " conspiracy," " theatre," " orator," &c.

The same natural aversion to loquacity has of late years made a very considerable alteration in our language, by closing in one syllable the termination of our preterperfect tense, as in the words "drown'd," "walk'd," "arriv'd," for "drowned," "walked," "arrived," which has very much disfigured the tongue, and turned a tenth part of our smoothest words into so many clusters of consonants. This is the more remarkable because the want of vowels in our language has been the general complaint of our politest authors, who nevertheless are the men that have made these retrenchments, and consequently very much increased our former scarcity.

This reflection on the words that end in "ed" I have heard in conversation from one of the greatest geniuses this age has produced. I think we may add to the foregoing observation, the change which has happened in our language by the abbreviation of several words that are terminated in "eth," by substituting an "s" in the room of the last syllable, as in "drowns," "walks," "arrives," and innumerable other words, which in the pronunciation of our forefathers were "drowneth," "walketh," "arriveth." This has wonderfully multiplied a letter which was before too frequent in the English tongue, and added to that hissing in our language which is taken so much notice of by foreigners, but at the same time humours our taciturnity, and eases us of many superfluous syllables.

I might here observe that the same single letter on many occasions does the office of a whole word, and represents the "his" and ·· her" of our forefathers. There is no doubt but the ear of a foreigner, which is the best judge in this case, would very much disapprove of such innovations, which indeed we do ourselves in some measure, by retaining the old termination in writing, and in all the solemn offices of our religion.

As, in the instances I have given, we have epitomised many of our particular words to the detriment of our tongue, so on other occasions we have drawn two words into one, which has likewise very much untuned our language, and clogged it with consonants, as "mayn't," "can't," "shan't," "won't," and the like, for ·· may not," "can not," "shall not," ·· will not," &c.

It is perhaps this humour of speaking no more than we needs must which has so miserably curtailed some of our words, that in familiar writings and conversations they often lose all but their first syllables, as in " mob.," " rep.," " pos.," " incog,," and the like; and as all ridiculous words make their first entry into a language by familiar phrases, I dare not answer for these that they will not in time be looked upon as a part of our tongue. We see some of our poets have been so indiscreet as to imitate Hudibras's doggrel expressions in their serious compositions. by throwing out the signs of our substantives which are essential to the English language. Nay, this humour of shortening our language had once run so far, that some of our celebrated authors, among whom we may reckon Sir Roger L'Estrange in particular, began to prune their words of all superfluous letters, as they termed them, in order to adjust the spelling to the pronunciation; which would have confounded all our etymologies, and have quite destroyed our tongue.

We may here likewise observe that our proper names, when familiarised in English, generally dwindle to monosyllables, whereas in other modern languages they receive a softer turn on this occasion, by the addition of a new syllable.—Nick, in Italian, is Nicolini; Jack, in French, Janot; and so of the rest.

There is another particular in our language which is a great instance of our frugality in words, and that is the suppressing of several particles which must be produced in other tongues to make a sentence intelligible. This often perplexes the best writers, when they find the relatives "whom," "which," or "they," at their mercy, whether they may have admission or not; and will never be decided till we have something like an academy, that by the best authorities, and rules drawn from the analogy of languages, shall settle all controversies between grammar and idiom.

I have only considered our language as it shows the genius and natural temper of the English, which is modest, thoughtful, and sincere, and which, perhaps, may recommend the people, though it has spoiled the tongue. We might, perhaps, carry the same thought into other languages, and deduce a great part of what is peculiar to them from the genius of the people who speak them. It is certain the light talkative humour of the French has not a little infected their tongue, which might be shown by many instances; as the genius of the Italians, which is so much addicted to music and ceremony, has moulded all their words and phrases to those particular uses. The stateliness and gravity of the Spaniards shows itself to perfection in the solemnity of their language; and the blunt, honest humour of the Germans sounds better in the roughness of the High-Dutch than it would in a politer tongue.

THE VISION OF MIRZA.

— Omnem, quæ nunc obducta tuenti
Mortales hebetat visus tibi, et humida circùm
Caligat, nubem eripiam.   VIRG., Æn. ii. 604.

.The cloud, which, intercepting the clear light,
Hangs o'er thy eyes, and blunts thy mortal sight,
I will remove.

WHEN I was at Grand Cairo, I picked up several Oriental manuscripts, which I have still by me. Among others I met with one entitled "The Visions of Mirza," which I have read over with great pleasure. I intend

to give it to the public when I have no other entertainment for them; and shall begin with the first
vision, which I have translated word for word as follows:

"On the fifth day of the moon, which, according to
the custom of my forefathers, I always keep holy,
after having washed myself, and offered up my morning devotions, I ascended the high hills of Bagdad, in
order to pass the rest of the day in meditation and
prayer. As I was here airing myself on the tops of
the mountains, I fell into a profound contemplation
on the vanity of human life; and passing from one
thought to another, 'Surely,' said I, 'man is but a
shadow, and life a dream.' Whilst I was thus musing,
I cast my eyes towards the summit of a rock that was
not far from me, where I discovered one in the habit
of a shepherd, with a musical instrument in his hand.
As I looked upon him he applied it to his lips, and
began to play upon it. The sound of it was exceeding
sweet, and wrought into a variety of tunes that were
inexpressibly melodious, and altogether different from
anything I had ever heard. They put me in mind of
those heavenly airs that are played to the departed
souls of good men upon their first arrival in Paradise,
to wear out the impressions of their last agonies, and
qualify them for the pleasures of that happy place.
My heart melted away in secret raptures.

"I had been often told that the rock before me was

the haunt of a genius, and that several had been entertained with music who had passed by it, but never
heard that the musician had before made himself
visible. When he had raised my thoughts by those
transporting airs which he played, to taste the pleasures
of his conversation, as I looked upon him like one
astonished, he beckoned to me, and, by the waving of
his hand, directed me to approach the place where he
sat. I drew near with that reverence which is due to
a superior nature; and, as my heart was entirely subdued by the captivating strains I had heard, I fell
down at his feet and wept. The genius smiled upon
me with a look of compassion and affability that
familiarised him to my imagination, and at once dis-
pelled all the fears and apprehensions with which I
approached him. He lifted me from the ground, and.
taking me by the hand, 'Mirza,' said he, 'I have heard
thee in thy soliloquies; follow me.'

"He then led me to the highest pinnacle of the rock,
and placing me on the top of it, 'Cast thy eyes east-
ward,' said he, 'and tell me what thou seest.' 'I see,'
said I. 'a huge valley, and a prodigious tide of water
rolling through it.' 'The valley that thou seest,' said
he, 'is the Vale of Misery, and the tide of water that
thou seest is part of the great tide of Eternity.' 'What
is the reason,' said I, 'that the tide I see rises out of a
thick mist at one end, and again loses itself in a thick
mist at the other?' 'What thou seest,' said he, 'is

that portion of Eternity which is called Time, measured out by the sun, and reaching from the beginning of the world to its consummation. Examine now,' said he, 'this sea that is bounded with darkness at both ends, and tell me what thou discoverest in it.' 'I see a bridge,' said I, 'standing in the midst of the tide.' 'The bridge thou seest,' said he, "is Human Life; consider it attentively.' Upon a more leisurely survey of it, I found that it consisted of threescore and ten entire arches, with several broken arches, which, added to those that were entire, made up the number about a hundred. As I was counting the arches, the genius told me that this bridge consisted at first of a thousand arches; but that a great flood swept away the rest, and left the bridge in the ruinous condition I now beheld it. 'But tell me further,' said he, 'what thou discoverest on it.' 'I see multitudes of people passing over it,' said I, 'and a black cloud hanging on each end of it.' As I looked more attentively, I saw several of the passengers dropping through the bridge into the great tide that flowed underneath it; and, upon further examination, perceived there were innumerable trap-doors that lay concealed in the bridge, which the passengers no sooner trod upon but they fell through them into the tide, and immediately disappeared These hidden pit-falls were set very thick at the entrance of the bridge, so that throngs of people no sooner broke through the cloud but many of them fell

THE VISION OF MIRZA.

into them. They grew thinner towards the middle.
but multiplied and lay closer together towards the end
of the arches that were entire.

"There were indeed some persons, but their number
was very small, that continued a kind of hobbling
march on the broken arches, but fell through one after
another, being quite tired and spent with so long a
walk.

"I passed some time in the contemplation of this
wonderful structure, and the great variety of objects
which it presented. My heart was filled with a deep
melancholy to see several dropping unexpectedly in the
midst of mirth and jollity, and catching at everything
that stood by them to save themselves. Some were
looking up towards the heavens in a thoughtful posture.
and in the midst of a speculation stumbled and fell out
of sight. Multitudes were very busy in the pursuit of
bubbles that glittered in their eyes and danced before
them; but often when they thought themselves within
the reach of them, their footing failed and down they
sunk. In this confusion of objects, I observed some
with scimitars in their hands, who ran to and fro
from the bridge, thrusting several persons on trap-
doors which did not seem to lie in their way, and
which they might have escaped had they not been
thus forced upon them.

"The genius, seeing me indulge myself on this
melancholy prospect, told me I had dwelt long enough

upon it. 'Take thine eyes off the bridge,' said he,
'and tell me if thou yet seest anything thou dost not
comprehend.' Upon looking up, 'What mean,' said I.
'those great flights of birds that are perpetnally
hovering about the bridge, and settling upon it from
time to time? I see vultures, harpies, ravens, cor-
morants, and among many other feathered creatures.
several little winged boys, that perch in great numbers
upon the middle arches.' 'These,' said the genius.
'are Envy, Avarice, Superstition, Despair, Love, with
the like cares and passions that infest human life.'

" I here fetched a deep sigh. 'Alas,' said I, 'man
was made in vain! how is he given away to misery
and mortality! tortured in life, and swallowed up in
death!' The genius, being moved with compassion
towards me, bade me quit so uncomfortable a prospect.
'Look no more,' said he, 'on man in the first stage of
his existence, in his setting out for Eternity; but cast
thine eye on that thick mist into which the tide bears
the several generations of mortals that fall into it.' I
directed my sight as I was ordered, and, whether or
no the good genius strengthened it with any supernatural force, or dissipated part of the mist that was
before too thick for the eye to penetrate, I saw the
valley opening at the further end, and spreading forth
into an immense ocean, that had a huge rock of
adamant running through the midst of it, and dividing
it into two equal parts. The clouds still rested on one

half of it, insomuch that I could discover nothing in
it; but the other appeared to me a vast ocean planted
with innumerable islands, that were covered with
fruits and flowers, and interwoven with a thousand
little shining seas that ran among them. I could see
persons dressed in glorious habits, with garlands upon
their heads, passing among the trees, lying down by
the sides of fountains, or resting on beds of flowers;
and could hear a confused harmony of singing birds.
falling waters, human voices, and musical instruments.
Gladness grew in me upon the discovery of so delightful a scene. I wished for the wings of an eagle, that
I might fly away to those happy seats; but the genius
told me there was no passage to them, except through the
gates of death that I saw opening every moment upon
the bridge. 'The islands.' said he, 'that lie so fresh
and green before thee, and with which the whole face
of the ocean appears spotted as far as thou canst see.
are more in number than the sands on the sea-shore:
there are myriads of islands behind those which thou
here discoverest, reaching further than thine eye, or
even thine imagination can extend itself. These are
the mansions of good men after death, who, according
to the degree and kinds of virtue in which they excelled.
are distributed among those several islands, which
abound with pleasures of different kinds and degrees,
suitable to the relishes and perfections of those who
are settled in them: every island is a paradise accom-

modated to its respective inhabitants. Are not these, O Mirza, habitations worth contending for? Does life appear miserable that gives thee opportunities of earning such a reward? Is death to be feared that will convey thee to so happy an existence? Think not man was made in vain, who has such an Eternity reserved for him." I gazed with inexpressible pleasure on these happy islands. At length, said I, 'Show me now, I beseech thee, the secrets that lie hid under those dark clouds which cover the ocean on the other side of the rock of adamant.' The genius making me no answer, I turned about to address myself to him a second time, but I found that he had left me; I then turned again to the vision which I had been so long contemplating: but instead of the rolling tide, the arched bridge, and the happy islands, I saw nothing but the long hollow valley of Bagdad, with oxen, sheep, and camels grazing upon the sides of it."

GENIUS.

—*Cui mens divinior, atque os*
Magna sonaturum des nominis hujus honorem.

HOR., *Sat.* i. 4, 43.

On him confer the poet's sacred name,
Whose lofty voice declares the heavenly flame.

THERE is no character more frequently given to a writer than that of being a genius. I have heard many a little sonneteer called a fine genius. There is not a heroic scribbler in the nation that has not his admirers who think him a great genius; and as for your smatterers in tragedy, there is scarce a man among them who is not cried up by one or other for a prodigious genius.

My design in this paper is to consider what is properly a great genius, and to throw some thoughts together on so uncommon a subject.

Among great geniuses those few draw the admiration of all the world upon them, and stand up as the prodigies of mankind, who, by the mere strength of natural parts, and without any assistance of art or learning, have produced works that were the delight of their own times and the wonder of posterity. There appears something nobly wild and extravagant in these great natural geniuses, that is infinitely more beautiful than all turn and polishing of what the French call a *bel esprit*, by which they would express a genius refined by conversation, reflection, and the reading of the most polite authors. The greatest genius which runs through the arts and sciences takes a kind of tincture from them and falls unavoidably into imitation.

Many of these great natural geniuses, that were never disciplined and broken by rules of art, are to be found among the ancients, and in particular among those of the more Eastern parts of the world. Homer has innumerable flights that Virgil was not able to reach, and in the Old Testament we find several passages more elevated and sublime than any in Homer. At the same time that we allow a greater and more daring genius to the ancients, we must own that the greatest of them very much failed in, or, if you will, that they were much above the nicety and correctness of the moderns. In their similitudes and allusions, provided there was a likeness, they did not much trouble themselves about the decency of the comparison : thus Solomon resembles the nose of his beloved to the tower of Lebanon which looketh towards Damascus, as the coming of a thief in the night is a similitude of the same kind in the New Testament. It would be endless to make collections of this nature. Homer illustrates one of his heroes encompassed with the enemy, by an ass in a field of corn that has his sides belaboured by all the boys of the village without stirring a foot for it ; and another of them tossing to and fro in his bed, and burning with resentment, to a piece of flesh broiled on the coals. This particular failure in the ancients opens a large field of raillery to the little wits, who can laugh at an indecency, but not relish the sublime in these sorts of writings. The present Emperor of Persia, conformable to this Eastern way of thinking, amidst a great many pompous titles, denominates himself "the sun of glory" and "the nutmeg of delight." In short, to cut off all cavilling against the ancients, and particularly those of the warmer climates, who had most heat and life in their imaginations, we are to consider that the rule of observing what the French call the *bienséance* in an allusion has been found out of later years, and in the colder regions of the world, where we could make some amends for our want of force and spirit by a scrupulous nicety and exactness in our compositions. Our countryman Shakespeare was a remarkable instance of this first kind of great geniuses.

I cannot quit this head without observing that Pindar was a great genius of the first class, who was hurried on by a natural fire and impetuosity to vast conceptions of things and noble sallies of imagination. At the same time can anything be more ridiculous than for men of a sober and moderate fancy to imitate this poet's way of writing in those monstrous compositions which go among us under the name of Pindarics? When I see people copying works which, as Horace has represented them, are singular in their kind, and inimitable; when I see men following irregularities by rule, and by the little tricks of art straining after the most unbounded flights of nature. I cannot but apply to them that passage in Terence :

—*Incerta hæc si tu postules*
Ratione certá facere, nihilo plus agas
Quâm si des operam, ut cum ratione insanias.

Eun., Act I., Sc. 1, l. 16.

You may as well pretend to be mad and in your senses at the same time, as to think of reducing these uncertain things to any certainty by reason.

In short, a modern Pindaric writer compared with Pindar is like a sister among the Camisars compared with Virgil's Sibyl; there is the distortion, grimace, and outward figure, but nothing of that divine impulse which raises the mind above itself, and makes the sounds more than human.

There is another kind of great geniuses which I shall place in a second class, not as I think them inferior to the first, but only for distinction's sake, as they are of a different kind. This second class of great geniuses are those that have formed themselves by rules, and submitted the greatness of their natural talents to the corrections and restraints of art. Such among the Greeks were Plato and Aristotle ; among the Romans. Virgil and Tully ; among the English, Milton and Sir Francis Bacon.

The genius in both these classes of authors may be equally great, but shows itself after a different manner.

In the first it is like a rich soil in a happy climate, that produces a whole wilderness of noble plants rising in a thousand beautiful landscapes without any certain order or regularity; in the other it is the same rich soil, under the same happy climate, that has been laid out in walks and parterres, and cut into shape and beauty by the skill of the gardener.

The great danger in these latter kind of geniuses is lest they cramp their own abilities too much by imitation, and form themselves altogether upon models, without giving the full play to their own natural parts. An imitation of the best authors is not to compare with a good original; and I believe we may observe that very few writers make an extraordinary figure in the world who have not something in their way of thinking or expressing themselves, that is peculiar to them, and entirely their own.

It is odd to consider what great geniuses are sometimes thrown away upon trifles.

"I once saw a shepherd," says a famous Italian author, "who used to divert himself in his solitudes with tossing up eggs and catching them again without breaking them; in which he had arrived to so great a degree of perfection that he would keep up four at a time for several minutes together playing in the air, and falling into his hand by turns. I think," says the author, "I never saw a greater severity than in this man's face, for by his wonderful perseverance and

application he had contracted the seriousness and
gravity of a privy councillor, and I could not but reflect with myself that the same assidnity and attention.
had they been rightly applied, 'might' have made a
greater mathematician than Archimedes."

THEODOSIUS AND CONSTANTIA.

Illa ; Quis et me, inquit, miseram, et te perdidit, Orpheu ?
Jamque vale : feror ingenti circumdata nocte,
Invalidasque tibi tendens, heu ! non tua, palmas.
              VIRG., *Georg.*, iv. 494.

Then thus the bride : " What fury seiz'd on thee,
Unhappy man ! to lose thyself and me ?—
And now farewell ! involv'd in shades of night,
For ever I am ravish'd from thy sight :
In vain I reach my feeble hands, to join
In sweet embraces—ah ! no longer thine ! " DRYDEN.

CONSTANTIA was a woman of extraordinary wit and
beauty, but very unhappy in a father who, having
arrived at great riches by his own industry, took
delight in nothing but his money. Theodosius was the
younger son of a decayed family, of great parts and
learning, improved by a genteel and virtuous education. When he was in the twentieth year of his age
he became acquainted with Constantia. who had not
then passed her fifteenth. As he lived but a few miles

distant from her father's house, he had frequent opportunities of seeing her; and, by the advantages of a
good person and a pleasing conversation, made such
an impression in her heart as it was impossible for
time to efface. He was himself no less smitten with
Constantia. A long acquaintance made them still
discover new beauties in each other, and by degrees
raised in them that mutual passion which had an
influence on their following lives. It unfortunately
happened that, in the midst of this intercourse of love
and friendship between Theodosius and Constantia,
there broke out an irreparable quarrel between their
parents; the one valuing himself too much upon his
birth, and the other upon his possessions. The father
of Constantia was so incensed at the father of Theodosius, that he contracted an unreasonable aversion
towards his son, insomuch that he forbade him his
house, and charged his daughter upon her duty never
to see him more. In the meantime, to break off all
communication between the two lovers, who he knew
entertained secret hopes of some favourable opportunity
that should bring them together, he found out a
young gentleman of a good fortune and an agreeable
person, whom he pitched upon as a husband for his
daughter. He soon concerted this affair so well, that
he told Constantia it was his design to marry her to
such a gentleman, and that her wedding should be
celebrated on such a day. Constantia, who was over-

awed with the authority of her father, and unable to object anything against so advantageous a match, received the proposal with a profound silence, which her father commended in her, as the most decent manner of a virgin's giving her consent to an overture of that kind. The noise of this intended marriage soon reached Theodosius, who, after a long tumult of passions which naturally rise in a lover's heart on such an occasion, wrote the following letter to Constantia :—

"The thought of my Constantia, which for some years has been my only happiness, is now become a greater torment to me than I am able to bear. Must I then live to see you another's? The streams, the fields, and meadows, where we have so often talked together, grow painful to me; life itself is become a burden. May you long be happy in the world, but forget that there was ever such a man in it as

"THEODOSIUS."

This letter was conveyed to Constantia that very evening, who fainted at the reading of it; and the next morning she was much more alarmed by two or three messengers that came to her father's house, one after another, to inquire if they had heard anything of Theodosius, who, it seems, had left his chamber about midnight, and could nowhere be found. The deep melancholy which had hung upon his mind some time before made them apprehend the worst that could befall him. Constantia, who knew that nothing but the report of her marriage could have driven him to such extremities, was not to be comforted. She now accused herself for having so tamely given an ear to the proposal of a husband, and looked upon the new lover as the murderer of. Theodosius. In short, she resolved to suffer the utmost effects of her father's displeasure rather than comply with a marriage which appeared to her so full of guilt and horror. The father, seeing himself entirely rid of Theodosius, and likely to keep a considerable portion in his family, was not very much concerned at the obstinate refusal of his daughter, and did not find it very difficult to excuse himself upon that account to his intended son-in-law, who had all along regarded this alliance rather as a marriage of convenience than of love. Constantia had now no relief but in her devotions and exercises of religion, to which her affections had so entirely subjected her mind, that after some years had abated the violence of her sorrows, and settled her thoughts in a kind of tranquillity, she resolved to pass the remainder of her days in a convent. Her father was not displeased with a resolution which would save money in his family, and readily complied with his daughter's intentions. Accordingly, in the twenty-fifth year of her age, while her beauty was yet in all its height and bloom, he carried her to a neighbouring city, in order to look out a sisterhood of nuns among whom to place his daughter.

There was in this place a father of a convent who was very much renowned for his piety and exemplary life: and as it is usual in the Romish Church for those who are under any great affliction, or trouble of mind, to apply themselves to the most eminent confessors for pardon and consolation, our beautiful votary took the opportunity of confessing herself to this celebrated father.

We must now return to Theodosius, who, the very morning that the above-mentioned inquiries had been made after him, arrived at a religious house in the city where now Constantia resided; and desiring that secrecy and concealment of the fathers of the convent, which is very usual upon any extraordinary occasion, he made himself one of the order, with a private vow never to inquire after Constantia; whom he looked upon as given away to his rival upon the day on which, according to common fame, their marriage was to have been solemnised. Having in his youth made a good progress in learning, that he might dedicate himself more entirely to religion, he entered into holy orders, and in a few years became renowned for his sanctity of life, and those pious sentiments which he inspired into all who conversed with him. It was this holy man to whom Constantia had determined to apply herself in confession, though neither she nor any other, besides the prior of the convent, knew anything of his name or family. The gay, the amiable Theodosius had now taken upon him the name of Father Francis, and was so far concealed in a long beard, a shaven head, and a religious habit, that it was impossible to discover the man of the world in the venerable conventual.

As he was one morning shut up in his confessional, Constantia kneeling by him opened the state of her soul to him ; and after having given him the history of a life full of innocence, she burst out into tears, and entered upon that part of her story in which he himself had so great a share. " My behaviour," says she, " has, I fear, been the death of a man who had no other fault but that of loving me too much. Heaven only knows how dear he was to me whilst he lived, and how bitter the remembrance of him has been to me since his death." She here paused, and lifted up her eyes that streamed with tears towards the father, who was so moved with the sense of her sorrows that he could only command his voice, which was broken with sighs and sobbings, so far as to bid her proceed. She followed his directions, and in a flood of tears poured out her heart before him. The father could not forbear weeping aloud, insomuch that, in the agonies of his grief, the seat shook under him. Constantia, who thought the good man was thus moved by his compassion towards her, and by the horror of her guilt, proceeded with the utmost contrition to acquaint him with that vow of virginity in which she was going to engage herself, as the proper atonement for her sins, and the only sacrifice she could make to the memory of Theodosius. The father, who by this time had pretty well composed himself, burst out again in tears upon hearing that name to which he had been so long disused, and upon receiving this instance of an unparalleled fidelity from one who he thought had several years since given herself up to the possession of another. Amidst the interruptions of his sorrow, seeing his penitent overwhelmed with grief, he was only able to bid her from time to time be comforted—to tell her that her sins were forgiven her—that her guilt was not so great as she apprehended—that she should not suffer herself to be afflicted above measure. After which he recovered himself enough to give her the absolution in form : directing her at the same time to repair to him again the next day, that he might encourage her in the pious resolution she had taken, and give her suitable exhortations for her behaviour in it. Constantia retired, and the next morning renewed her applications. Theodosius, having manned his soul with proper thoughts and reflections, exerted himself on this occasion in the best manner he could to animate his penitent in the course of life she was entering upon, and wear out of her mind those groundless fears and apprehensions which had taken possession of it ; concluding with a promise to her, that he would from time to time continue his admonitions when she should have taken upon her the holy veil. " The rules of our respective orders," says he, " will not permit that I should see you ; but you may assure yourself not only of having a place in my prayers, but of receiving such frequent instructions as I can convey to you by letters. Go on cheerfully in the glorious course you have undertaken, and you will quickly find such a peace and satisfaction in your mind which it is not in the power of the world to give."

Constantia's heart was so elevated with the discourse of Father Francis, that the very next day she entered upon her vow. As soon as the solemnities of her reception were over, she retired, as it is usual, with the abbess into her own apartment.

The abbess had been informed the night before of all that had passed between her novitiate and father Francis : from whom she now delivered to her the following letter :—

" As the first-fruits of those joys and consolations which you may expect from the life you are now engaged in, I must acquaint you that Theodosius, whose death sits so heavy upon your thoughts, is still alive; and that the father to whom you have confessed yourself was once that Theodosius whom you so much lament. The love which we have had for one another will make us more happy in its disappointment than it could have done in its success. Providence has disposed of us for our advantage, though not according to our wishes. Consider your Theodosius still as dead,

but assure yourself of one who will not cease to pray
for you in father   "FRANCIS."

Constantia saw that the handwriting agreed with
the contents of the letter; and, upon reflecting on the
voice of the person, the behaviour, and above all the
extreme sorrow of the father during her confession, she
discovered Theodosius in every particular. After
having wept with tears of joy, "It is enough," says
she; "Theodosius is still in being: I shall live with
comfort and die in peace."

The letters which the father sent her afterwards are
yet extant in the nunnery where she resided; and are
often read to the young religious, in order to inspire
them with good resolutions and sentiments of virtue.
It so happened that after Constantia had lived about
ten years in the cloister, a violent fever broke out in
the place, which swept away great multitudes, and
among others Theodosius. Upon his death-bed he sent
his benediction in a very moving manner to Constantia,
who at that time was herself so far gone in the same
fatal distemper that she lay delirious. Upon the interval
which generally precedes death in sickness of this
nature, the abbess, finding that the physicians had
given her over, told her that Theodosius had just gone
before her, and that he had sent her his benediction in
his last moments. Constantia received it with pleasure.
"And now," says she, "if I do not ask anything

improper, let me be buried by Theodosius. My vow reaches no further than the grave; what I ask is, I hope, no violation of it." She died soon after, and was interred according to her request.

The tombs are still to be seen, with a short Latin inscription over them to the following purpose :—

" Here lie the bodies of Father Francis and Sister Constance. They were lovely in their lives, and in their death they were not divided."

GOOD NATURE.

Sic vita erat : facilè omnes perferre ac pati :
Cum quibus erat cunque unà, his sese dedere,
Eorum obsequi studiis : advorsus nemini ;
Nunquam præponens se aliis. Ita facillime
Sine invidia invenias laudem.—

TER., *Andr.*, *Act* i. sc. 1.

His manner of life was this : to bear with everybody's humours; to comply with the inclinations and pursuits of those he conversed with; to contradict nobody; never to assume a superiority over others. This is the ready way to gain applause without exciting envy.

MAN is subject to innumerable pains and sorrows by the very condition of humanity, and yet, as if Nature had not sown evils enough in life, we are continually adding grief to grief, and aggravating the common calamity by our cruel treatment of one another. Every man's natural weight of affliction is still made more heavy by the envy, malice, treachery, or injustice of his neighbour. At the same time that the storm beats on the whole species, we are falling foul upon one another.

Half the misery of human life might be extinguished, would men alleviate the general curse they lie under, by mutual offices of compassion, benevolence, and humanity. There is nothing, therefore, which we ought more to encourage in ourselves and others, than that disposition of mind which in our language goes under the title of good nature, and which I shall choose for the subject of this day's speculation.

Good nature is more agreeable in conversation than wit, and gives a certain air to the countenance which is more amiable than beauty. It shows virtue in the fairest light, takes off in some measure from the deformity of vice, and makes even folly and impertinence supportable.

There is no society or conversation to be kept up in the world without good nature, or something which must bear its appearance, and supply its place. For this reason, mankind have been forced to invent a kind of artificial humanity, which is what we express by the word good-breeding. For if we examine thoroughly the idea of what we call so, we shall find it to be nothing else but an imitation and mimicry of good nature, or, in other terms, affability, complaisance, and easiness of temper, reduced into an art. These exterior shows and appearances of humanity render a man wonderfully popular and beloved, when they are founded upon a real good nature; but, without it, are like hypocrisy in religion, or a bare form of holiness, which, when it is discovered, makes a man more detestable than professed impiety.

Good-nature is generally born with us: health, prosperity, and kind treatment from the world, are great cherishers of it where they find it; but nothing is capable of forcing it up, where it does not grow of itself. It is one of the blessings of a happy constitution, which education may improve, but not produce.

Xenophon, in the life of his imaginary prince whom he describes as a pattern for real ones, is always celebrating the philanthropy and good nature of his hero, which he tells us he brought into the world with him; and gives many remarkable instances of it in his childhood, as well as in all the several parts of his life. Nay, on his death-bed, he describes him as being pleased, that while his soul returned to Him who made it, his body should incorporate with the great mother of all things, and by that means become beneficial to mankind. For which reason, he gives his sons a positive order not to enshrine it in gold or silver, but to lay it in the earth as soon as the life was gone out of it.

An instance of such an overflowing of humanity, such an exuberant love to mankind, could not have entered into the imagination of a writer who had not a soul filled with great ideas, and a general bene-volence to mankind.

In that celebrated passage of Sallust, where Cæsar and Cato are placed in such beautiful but opposite lights, Cæsar's character is chiefly made up of good nature, as it showed itself in all its forms towards his friends or his enemies, his servants or dependents, the guilty or the distressed. As for Cato's character, it is rather awful than amiable. Justice seems most agreeable to the nature of God. and mercy to that of man. A Being who has nothing to pardon in Himself, may reward every man according to his works; but he whose very best actions must be seen with grains of allowance, cannot be too mild, moderate, and forgiving. For this reason. among all the monstrous characters in human nature. there is none so odious, nor indeed so exquisitely ridiculous, as that of a rigid, severe temper in a worth-less man.

This part of good nature however, which consists in the pardoning and overlooking of faults, is to be exercised only in doing ourselves justice, and that too in the ordinary commerce and occurrences of life;

for, in the public administrations of justice, mercy to one may be cruelty to others.

It is grown almost into a maxim, that good-natured men are not always men of the most wit. This observation, in my opinion, has no foundation in nature. The greatest wits I have conversed with are men eminent for their humanity. I take, therefore, this remark to have been occasioned by two reasons. First, because ill-nature among ordinary observers passes for wit. A spiteful saying gratifies so many little passions in those who hear it, that it generally meets with a good reception. The laugh rises upon it, and the man who utters it is looked upon as a shrewd satirist. This may be one reason why a great many pleasant companions appear so surprisingly dull when they have endeavoured to be merry in print ; the public being more just than private clubs or assemblies, in distinguishing between what is wit and what is ill-nature.

Another reason why the good-natured man may sometimes bring his wit in question is perhaps because he is apt to be moved with compassion for those misfortunes or infirmities which another would turn into ridicule, and by that means gain the reputation of a wit. The ill-natured man, though but of equal parts, gives himself a larger field to expatiate in ; he exposes those failings in human nature which the other would cast a veil over, laughs at vices which the other either excuses or conceals, gives utterance to reflections which the other stifles, falls indifferently upon friends or enemies, exposes the person who has . obliged him, and, in short, sticks at nothing that may establish his character as a wit. It is no wonder, therefore, he succeeds in it better than the man of humanity, as a person who makes use of indirect methods is more likely to grow rich than the fair trader.

———————

— Quis enim bonus, aut face dignus
Arcani, qualem Cereris vult esse sacerdos,
Ulla aliena sibi credat mala ! —

JUV., *Sat.* xv. 140.

Who can all sense of others' ills escape,
Is but a brute, at best, in human shape.

TATE.

IN one of my last week's papers, I treated of good-nature as it is the effect of constitution; I shall now speak of it as it is a moral virtue. The first may make a man easy in himself and agreeable to others, but implies no merit in him that is possessed of it. A man is no more to be praised upon this account, than because he has a regular pulse or a good digestion. This good nature, however, in the constitution, which Mr. Dryden somewhere calls "a milkiness of blood," is an admirable groundwork for the other. In order, therefore, to try our good-nature, whether it arises from the body or the mind, whether it be founded in the animal or rational part of our nature; in a word, whether it be such as is entitled to any other reward besides that secret satisfaction and contentment of mind which is essential to it, and the kind reception it procures us in the world, we must examine it by the following rules:

First, whether it acts with steadiness and uniformity in sickness and in health, in prosperity and in adversity; if otherwise, it is to be looked upon as nothing else but an irradiation of the mind from some new supply of spirits, or a more kindly circulation of the blood. Sir Francis Bacon mentions a cunning solicitor, who would never ask a favour of a great man before dinner; but took care to prefer his petition at a time when the party petitioned had his mind free from care, and his appetites in good humour. Such a transient temporary good-nature as this, is not that philanthropy, that love of mankind, which deserves the title of a moral virtue.

The next way of a man's bringing his good-nature to the test is to consider whether it operates according to the rules of reason and duty: for if, notwithstanding its general benevolence to mankind, it makes no distinction between its objects; if it exerts itself promiscuously towards the deserving and the undeserving; if it relieves alike the idle and the indigent; if it gives itself up to the first petitioner, and lights upon any one rather by accident than choice—it may pass for an amiable instinct, but must not assume the name of a moral virtue.

The third trial of good-nature will be the examining ourselves whether or no we are able to exert it to our own disadvantage, and employ it on proper objects, notwithstanding any little pain, want, or inconvenience, which may arise to ourselves from it: in a word, whether we are willing to risk any part of our fortune, our reputation, our health or ease. for the benefit of mankind. Among all these expressions of good nature, I shall single out that which goes under the general name of charity, as it consists in relieving the indigent: that being a trial of this kind which offers itself to us almost at all times and in every place.

I should propose it as a rule, to every one who is provided with any competency of fortune more than sufficient for the necessaries of life, to lay aside a certain portion of his income for the use of the poor. This I would look upon as an offering to Him who has a right to the whole, for the use of those whom. in the passage hereafter mentioned, He has described as His own representatives upon earth. At the same time, we should manage our charity with such prudence and caution, that we may not hurt our own friends or relations whilst we are doing good to those who are strangers to us.

This may possibly be explained better by an example than by a rule.

Eugenius is a man of a universal good nature, and generous beyond the extent of his fortune; but withal so prudent in the economy of his affairs, that what goes out in charity is made up by good management. Eugenius has what the world calls two hundred pounds a year; but never values himself above nine-score, as not thinking he has a right to the tenth part, which he always appropriates to charitable uses. To this sum he frequently makes other voluntary additions, insomuch, that in a good year—for such he accounts those in which he has been able to make greater bounties than ordinary—he has given above twice that sum to the sickly and indigent. Eugenius prescribes to himself many particular days of fasting and abstinence, in order to increase his private bank of charity, and sets aside what would be the current expenses of those times for the use of the poor. He often goes afoot where his business calls him, and at the end of his walk has given a shilling, which in his ordinary methods of expense would have gone for coach-hire, to the first necessitous person that has fallen in his way. I have known him, when he has been going to a play or an opera, divert the money which was designed for that purpose upon an object of charity whom he has met with in the street; and afterwards pass his evening in a coffee-house, or at a friend's fireside, with much greater satisfaction to himself than he could have received from the most exquisite entertainments of the theatre. By these means he is generous without impoverishing himself, and enjoys his estate by making it the property of others.

There are few men so cramped in their private affairs, who may not be charitable after this manner, without any disadvantage to themselves, or prejudice to their families. It is but sometimes sacrificing a diversion or convenience to the poor, and turning the usual course of our expenses into a better channel. This is, I think, not only the most prudent and convenient, but the most meritorious piece of charity which we can put in practice. By this method, we in some measure share the necessities of the poor at the same time that we relieve them, and make ourselves not only their patrons, but their fellow-sufferers.

Sir Thomas Brown, in the last part of his "Religio Medici," in which he describes his charity in several heroic instances, and with a noble heat of sentiments, mentions that verse in the Proverbs of Solomon : " He that giveth to the poor lendeth to the Lord." There is more rhetoric in that one sentence, says he, than in a library of sermons ; and indeed, if those sentences were understood by the reader with the same emphasis as they are delivered by the author, we needed not those volumes of instructions, but might be honest by an epitome.

This passage of Scripture is, indeed, wonderfully persuasive ; but I think the same thought is carried much further in the New Testament, where our Saviour

tells us, in a most pathetic manner, that he shall
hereafter regard the clothing of the naked, the feeding
of the hungry, and the visiting of the imprisoned, as
offices done to Himself, and reward them accordingly.
Pursuant to those passages in Holy Scripture, I have
somewhere met with the epitaph of a charitable man,
which has very much pleased me. I cannot recollect
the words, but the sense of it is to this purpose : What
I spent I lost ; what I possessed is left to others ; what
I gave away remains with me.

Since I am thus insensibly engaged in Sacred Writ,
I cannot forbear making an extract of several passages
which I have always read with great delight in the
book of Job. It is the account which that holy man
gives of his behaviour in the days of his prosperity;
and, if considered only as a human composition, is a
finer picture of a charitable and good-natured man
than is to be met with in any other author.

" Oh that I were as in months past, as in the days
when God preserved me : When his candle shined
upon my head, and when by his light I walked through
darkness : When the Almighty was yet with me ; when
my children were about me : When I washed my steps
with butter, and the rock poured me out rivers of oil.

" When the ear heard me, then it blessed me ; and
when the eye saw me, it gave witness to me. Because
I delivered the poor that cried, and the fatherless, and
him that had none to help him. The blessing of him

that was ready to perish came upon me, and I caused
the widow's heart to sing for joy. I was eyes to the
blind; and feet was I to the lame; I was a father to
the poor, and the cause which I knew not I searched
out. Did not I weep for him that was in trouble?
Was not my soul grieved for the poor? Let me be
weighed in an even balance, that God may know mine
integrity. If I did despise the cause of my man-
servant or of my maid-servant when they contended
with me: What then shall I do when God riseth up?
and when he visiteth, what shall I answer him? Did
not he that made me in the womb, make him? and did
not one fashion us in the womb? If I have withheld
the poor from their desire, or have caused the eyes of
the widow to fail; Or have eaten my morsel myself
alone, and the fatherless hath not eaten thereof; If I
have seen any perish for want of clothing, or any poor
without covering; If his loins have not blessed me,
and if he were not warmed with the fleece of my
sheep; If I have lifted my hand against the fatherless,
when I saw my help in the gate: Then let mine arm
fall from my shoulder-blade, and mine arm be broken
from the bone. If I [have] rejoiced at the destruction
of him that hated me, or lifted up myself when evil
found him: Neither have I suffered my mouth to sin,
by wishing a curse to his soul. The stranger did
not lodge in the street; but I opened my doors to the
traveller. If my land cry against me, or that the

furrows likewise thereof complain : If I have eaten
the fruits thereof without money, or have caused the
owners thereof to lose their life : Let thistles grow
instead of wheat. and cockle instead of barley."

A GRINNING MATCH.

—*Remove fera monstra, tuaque*
Saxificos vultus, quæcunque ea, tolle Medusæ.

OVID, *Met.* v. 216.

Hence with those monstrous features, and, O ! spare
That Gorgon's look, and petrifying stare.   POPE.

IN a late paper, I mentioned the project of an ingenious author for the erecting of several handicraft
prizes to be contended for by our British artisans, and
the influence they might have towards the improve-
ment of our several manufactures. I have since that
been very much surprised by the following advertise-
ment, which I find in the *Post-boy* of the 11th instant,
and again repeated in the *Post-boy* of the 15th :—

" On the 9th of October next will be run for upon
Coleshill-heath, in Warwickshire, a plate of six guineas
value, three heats, by any horse, mare, or gelding that
hath not won above the value of £5, the winning horse
to be sold for £10, to carry 10 stone weight. if 14 hands
high ; if above or under, to carry or be allowed weight

for inches, and to be entered Friday, the 5th, at the Swan in Coleshill, before six in the evening. Also, a plate of less value to be run for by asses. The same day a gold ring to be grinn'd for by men."

The first of these diversions that is to be exhibited by the £10 race-horses, may probably have its use; but the two last, in which the asses and men are concerned, seem to me altogether extraordinary and unaccountable. Why they should keep running asses at Coleshill, or how making mouths turns to account in Warwickshire, more than in any other parts of England, I cannot comprehend. I have looked over all the Olympic games, and do not find anything in them like an ass-race, or a match at grinning. However it be, I am informed that several asses are now kept in body-clothes, and sweated every morning upon the heath : and that all the country-fellows within ten miles of the Swan grin an hour or two in their glasses every morning, in order to qualify themselves for the 9th of October. The prize which is proposed to be grinned for has raised such an ambition among the common people of out-grinning one another, that many very discerning persons are afraid it should spoil most of the faces in the county; and that a Warwickshire man will be known by his grin, as Roman Catholics imagine a Kentish man is by his tail. The gold ring which is made the prize of deformity, is just the reverse of the golden apple that was formerly made

the prize of beauty, and should carry for its poesy the
old motto inverted :

.   *Detur tetriori.*

Or, to accommodate it to the capacity of the combatants,

The frightfull'st grinner
Be the winner.

In the meanwhile I would advise a Dutch painter to
be present at this great controversy of faces, in order
to make a collection of the most remarkable grins that
shall be there exhibited.

I must not here omit an account which I lately received of one of these grinning matches from a gentleman, who, upon reading the above-mentioned advertise-
ment, entertained a coffee-house with the following
narrative :—Upon the taking of Namur, amidst other
public rejoicings made on that occasion, there was a
gold ring given by a Whig justice of peace to be
grinned for. The first competitor that entered the
lists was a black, swarthy Frenchman, who accidentally
passed that way, and being a man naturally of a
withered look and hard features, promised himself
good success. He was placed upon a table in the
great point of view, and, looking upon the company
like Milton's Death,

Grinned horribly a ghastly smile.

His muscles were so drawn together on each side of
his face that he showed twenty teeth at a grin, and put

the country in some pain lest a foreigner should carry away the honour of the day: but upon a further trial they found he was master only of the merry grin.

The next that mounted the table was a malcontent in those days, and a great master in the whole art of grinning, but particularly excelled in the angry grin. He did his part so well that he is said to have made half a dozen women miscarry; but the justice being apprised by one who stood near him that the fellow who grinned in his face was a Jacobite, and being unwilling that a disaffected person should win the gold ring, and be looked upon as the best grinner in the county, he ordered the oaths to be tendered unto him upon his quitting the table, which the grinner refusing, he was set aside as an unqualified person. There were several other grotesque figures that presented themselves, which it would be too tedious to describe. I must not, however, omit a ploughman, who lived in the further part of the county, and being very lucky in a pair of long lantern jaws, wrung his face into such a hideous grimace that every feature of it appeared under a different distortion. The whole company stood astonished at such a complicated grin, and were ready to assign the prize to him, had it not been proved by one of his antagonists that he had practised with verjuice for some days before, and had a crab found upon him at the very time of grinning; upon which the best judges of grinning declared it as their opinion that he was not to be looked upon as a fair grinner, and therefore ordered him to be set aside as a cheat.

The prize, it seems, fell at length upon a cobbler, Giles Gorgon by name, who produced several new grins of his own invention, having been used to cut faces for many years together over his last. At the very first grin he cast every human feature out of his countenance; at the second he became the face of a spout; at the third a baboon; at the fourth the head of a bass-viol; and at the fifth a pair of nut-crackers. The whole assembly wondered at his accomplishments, and bestowed the ring on him unanimously; but what he esteemed more than all the rest, a country wench, whom he had wooed in vain for above five years before, was so charmed with his grins and the applauses which he received on all sides, that she married him the week following, and to this day wears the prize upon her finger, the cobbler having made use of it as his wedding ring.

This paper might perhaps seem very impertinent if it grew serious in the conclusion. I would, neverthe-less, leave it to the consideration of those who are the patrons of this monstrous trial of skill, whether or no they are not guilty, in some measure, of an affront to their species in treating after this manner the "human face divine," and turning that part of us, which has so great an image impressed upon it, into the image of a monkey; whether the raising such silly competitions among the ignorant, proposing prizes for such useless accomplishments, filling the common people's heads with such senseless ambitions, and inspiring them with such absurd ideas of superiority and pre-eminence, has not in it something immoral as well as ridiculous.

TRUST IN GOD.

Si fractus illabatur orbis,
Imparidum ferient ruinœ.

— Hor., *Car.* iii. 3, 7.

Should the whole frame of nature round him break,
 In ruin and confusion hurled,
He, unconcerned, would hear the mighty crack,
 And stand secure amidst a falling world.   Anon.

MAN, considered in himself, is a very helpless and a very wretched being. He is subject every moment to the greatest calamities and misfortunes. He is beset with dangers on all sides, and may become unhappy by numberless casualties which he could not foresee, nor have prevented had he foreseen them.

It is our comfort, while we are obnoxious to so many accidents, that we are under the care of One who directs contingencies, and has in His hands the management of everything that is capable of annoying or offending us;

who knows the assistance we stand in need of, and is always ready to bestow it on those who ask it of Him.

The natural homage which such a creature bears to so infinitely wise and good a Being is a firm reliance on Him for the blessings and conveniences of life, and an habitual trust in Him for deliverance out of all such dangers and difficulties as may befall us.

The man who always lives in this disposition of mind has not the same dark and melancholy views of human nature as he who considers himself abstractedly from this relation to the Supreme Being. At the same time that he reflects upon his own weakness and imperfection he comforts himself with the contemplation of thos Divine attributes which are employed for his sa ty and his welfare. He finds his want of foresight m ... up by the Omniscience of Him who is his sup- p He is not sensible of his own want of strength w he knows that his helper is almighty. In short, th person who has a firm trust on the Supreme Being is powerful in His power, wise by His wisdom, happy by His happiness. He reaps the benefit of every D ne attribute, and loses his own insufficiency in the fu ss of infinite perfection.

make our lives more easy to us, we are commanded t our trust in Him, who is thus able to relieve and ur us; the Divine goodness having made such r nce a du y, notwithstanding we should have been m able l d it been forbidden us.

Among several motives which might be made use of to recommend this duty to us, I shall only take notice of those that follow.

The first and strongest is, that we are promised He will not fail those who put their trust in Him.

But without considering the supernatural blessing which accompanies this duty, we may observe that it has a natural tendency to its own reward, or, in other words, that this firm trust and confidence in the great Disposer of all things contributes very much to the getting clear of any affliction, or to the bearing it manfully. A person who believes he has his succour at hand, and that he acts in the sight of his friend, often exerts himself beyond his abilities, and does wonders that are not to be matched by one who is not animated with such a confidence of success. I could produce instances from history of generals who, out of a belief that they were under the protection of some invisible assistant, did not only encourage their soldiers to do their utmost, but have acted themselves beyond what they would have done had they not been inspired by such a belief. I might in the same manner show how such a trust in the assistance of an Almighty Being naturally produces patience, hope, cheerfulness, and all other dispositions of the mind that alleviate those calamities which we are not able to remove.

The practice of this virtue administers great comfort to the mind of man in times of poverty and affliction, but most of all in the hour of death. When the soul is hovering in the last moments of its separation, when it is just entering on another state of existence, to converse with scenes, and objects, and companions, that are altogether new—what can support her under such tremblings of thought, such fear, such anxiety, such apprehensions, but the casting of all her cares upon Him who first gave her being, who has conducted her through one stage of it, and will be always with her, to guide and comfort her in her progress through eternity?

David has very beautifully represented this steady reliance on God Almighty in his twenty-third Psalm, which is a kind of pastoral hymn, and filled with those allusions which are usual in that kind of writing. As the poetry is very exquisite, I shall present my reader with the following translation of it:

I.

The Lord my pasture shall prepare,
And feed me with a shepherd's care;
His presence shall my wants supply,
And guard me with a watchful eye;
My noonday walks He shall attend,
And all my midnight hours defend.

II.

When in the sultry glebe I faint,
Or on the thirsty mountain pant;
To fertile vales and dewy meads
My weary, wand'ring steps He leads;
Where peaceful rivers, soft and slow,
Amid the verdant landscape flow.

III.

Though in the paths of death I tread,
With gloomy horrors overspread,
My steadfast heart shall fear no ill,
For thou, O Lord, art with me still ;
Thy friendly crook shall give me aid,
And guide me through the dreadful shade.

IV.

Though in a bare and rugged way,
Through devious, lonely wilds I stray,
Thy bounty shall my pains beguile :
The barren wilderness shall smile
With sudden greens and herbage crowned,
And streams shall murmur all around.

www.ingramcontent.com/pod-product-compliance
Lightning Source LLC
Chambersburg PA
CBHW030559040726
47497CB00008B/2795